Night OF THE
Amber
Moon

T U L S A

ISBN: 978-1954095-52-6
Night of the Amber Moon

Yorkshire Publishing
1425 E 41st Pl
Tulsa, OK 74105
www.YorkshirePublishing.com
918.394.2665

Published in the USA

Night OF THE Amber Moon

HELEN DUNLAP NEWTON

DEDICATION

NIGHT OF THE AMBER MOON is dedicated to Merle Newton, who always encouraged me to go for my dreams, and to Anna Myers who took me and so many others under her writing wings.

ACKNOWLEDGEMENTS

Thank you to the Society of Children's Book Writers and Illustrators and especially my SCBWI-Oklahoma Region. Someone told me 20 years ago, "If you are serious about writing for children, join SCBWI." They were so right.

I also have to thank my numerous critique friends. You read bits and pieces of many versions and helped me carve out the real story.

How can I write a story like this and not thank my brother, Paul and my sister, Betty? This story is not about us, but they were the inspiration for the siblings watching out for their little sister.

CHAPTER 1

I f it weren't for the cell tower near the cemetery, visitors would swear the town was a 1950's village—only emerging from the mist when the time was right. On its postage-stamp plot of earth, bisected by train tracks and surrounded by cornfields, Taggert Creek kept its secrets hidden. Some said the town was boring. Others thought something else.

Peaceful.

Contented.

Happy.

But none of those words defined the girl sitting with her friends in the back row of the bus as it stopped in front of her parents' feed store.

This girl studied faces.

This girl dreaded finding empty liquor bottles in the trash bin beside the store.

This girl let out the breath she didn't even realize she'd been holding.

Dad's truck was gone.

"Good," she whispered.

"Good what?" Ariel asked, then nudged Izzy with her shoulder.

"Uh...good, I got a B- on my math test." Izzy searched Ariel's face for a reaction, but Mrs. Mackelhaney's scratchy voice distracted her.

"Hurry it up, Isabel Dunn. Got to get this bus back by four."

Izzy scrunched up her face and shouted, "Izzy! My name is Izzy."

Ariel grabbed her arm. "Don't forget. Ask about your birthday as soon as you see your mom."

"Yeah. Don't chicken out," Jody added from the other side of Ariel.

"Bawk, bawk!" Izzy flapped her arms like a chicken—trying to cover the pressure she felt from her friends. Her forehead crinkled. "I...I'll try. It depends."

"Today," Ariel demanded, then smiled and pushed Izzy from the seat.

The bus horn honked, and Mrs. Mackelhaney did a whirling thing with her finger.

"Sorry. Be right there." Izzy inched through the maze of legs in the aisle then focused on the bus driver's face in the mirror.

Mrs. Mackelhaney growled into the reflection, "Isabel's a good name. It's my own grandmother's name."

"Exactly." Izzy mumbled.

Ariel and Jody called from the back seat, "Today!" Their laughter made Izzy wince behind her smile. She was tempted to go back and ride the rest of the route with them. Instead, she raised her thumb in fake agreement, then hopped from the bus steps to the sidewalk.

Jody was right. Izzy hated asking Mom for stuff. She'd been promising she'd ask about her birthday for weeks, but Ariel and Jody didn't get it. She couldn't just ask. It was about more than a birthday. The timing had to be right. Ariel kept pushing her for a slumber party—almost planning it. Izzy shook her head and turned to wave. She smiled when her friends made dorky faces through the back window. The bus roared away, leaving her alone and coughing in a cloud of diesel fumes.

A cold breeze scuttled along Park Street and cleared the air. It pushed at her. She shivered inside the coat of her dad's she'd grabbed by mistake that morning. The smell of cigarettes and his musky scent filled her head and made her nose wrinkle. She turned to blink grit from her lashes, then stuffed her tangled hair under the hood. Instead of heading straight into the store's office, she angled to the left, hoping to snatch a few minutes of reading in the store's feed storage building next door.

On the other side of the feed building, the wind swirled the tarnished weathervane on the roof of the old abandoned brick theater. Izzy stared at the metal version of a regal-looking cat squeaking on top of the pole.

She shuddered.

The rattling and other sounds coming from behind those brick walls always gave her the creeps—squeaking doors, wings fluttering from the roof's tower. And then there was the thumping that echoed deep inside the empty building.

She had first heard it with her brother, Michael.

"Don't freak," he had said. "It's just a door blowing in the wind," She had believed him, even though his eye twitched.

He hadn't told her the rest, though.

Hadn't shared the town legend about the ghost of Dirty Bertie.

But Jody did.

"They say she thumps through the theater with her broom, looking for her lost love," Jody had whispered at a sleepover in fifth grade.

Someone had squealed. Someone had said, "Let's find a way in and see her ghost."

And they'd tried.

Over and over.

But the back door was always locked tight.

Izzy itched to add words to her theater story in the spiral notebook she hid under her pillow. She pictured the scene—her flashlight beam making tracks in the dusty air—Ariel and Jody begging her to go first.

She was the brave one.

In her stories.

In the real world, not so much.

The wind grew stronger. She leaned against it as it pushed at her like an invisible hand shoving her toward the theater. She imagined a vast room, dark and musty. A slanted floor and her feet slipping and sliding past hundreds of cold and empty seats. The smell of decay filling her nose and throat until she choked. Remembering the nightmare triggered a thousand prickles through her body and one of her greatest fears.

What would she do if the back door ever opened?

A rap on the side window of the feed store office made her jump. She willed her heart to slow its racing and her breathing to steady. No question why Mom was frowning through the glass. She had said the theater was off-limits right after Dunn's Feed & Seed opened a year ago.

Izzy dropped her shoulders in one big sigh, then counted her steps to the office building and opened the door. Tension snapped in the air like static after touching metal.

"You don't understand, Mom." Izzy's older sister said. "I have to do this. No one from Taggert Creek has ever competed in the Kansas Math Olympiad!"

"Sorry, Beth, we can't afford it." Mom pounded the keys on the computer. "Izzy, put your things in the back room, not on the couch," she said, using the Jedi-mom trick of knowing without seeing.

Beth rolled her eyes, and Izzy stuck out her tongue at her sister—their typical communication. Beth turned back to their mom. "I think the school pays for most of it."

"We'll see," Mom said, which probably meant no. "Izzy, after you put your bag up, go see if your brother has finished stacking the feed next door." Mom glanced at the clock. "Your dad wasn't feeling good when he went on the feed delivery. Should've been back by now." She ran her hand through her short hair. "You kids don't need to bother him tonight."

Izzy glanced at Beth. Her sister's face mirrored the same dread she felt—color-drained, eyes darting back and forth. One sister biting her lip, the other biting her nails.

Mom gathered papers from the counter. "I'm closing up early to start supper."

Anxious to escape, Izzy tossed her bag, causing it to skid across the cement floor and Maverick to startle from his blanket on the floor.

Izzy kneeled to pet the dog's long ears. "Sorry, Maverick. How come Dad didn't take you with him?" She walked into the back room and hung Dad's coat on a hook. Grabbing her own jacket, she hurried out the door, glad to escape Beth's sad face and mom's pounding fingers on the computer keys.

The sun's last horizontal rays peaked through the trees in the park across the street. Taggert Creek was closing for the night, with pickups roaring their way home and streetlights buzzing to life.

Izzy felt a throbbing in her chest from the bass of her brother's music in the feed storage building between the office and the theater. Michael was probably running sprints between the long rows of stacked bags of feed. She glanced in the trash bin beside the office— one empty bottle—three scrunched beer cans.

She opened the storage-building door and pulled the neck of her sweatshirt over her nose to mask the stink of animal feed and sweat. The air was cool inside the building, but the heat from Michael's body rushed past her with each of his laps.

"Michael," Izzy shouted through the fabric. He smiled as he kept running. He flipped the hood of her jacket over the top of her head when he slid around the corner.

Izzy pressed the stop button on the music to get his attention.

"Hey, what'd you do that for, Isabel?" He pulled the front end of his shirt up to wipe his face and leaned against bags of horse feed.

She let go of her shirt's neck and tried to breathe through her mouth. "Don't call me that. Mom said she's closing early. You beat your time?"

Michael dropped to the floor and grunted with each push-up. "Shaved off three seconds. Got two weeks till tryouts."

"You ask Mom about the running shoes yet?"

Chances for even the smallest celebration on her birthday were not looking good with Beth's math thing and Michael needing running shoes.

Five more push-ups, then Michael jumped to his feet. "Nah, haven't found the right time. How come she's closing early?"

Izzy shrugged her shoulders, "She said Dad wasn't feeling good, and now he's late."

Biting into the edge of her thumbnail, she said, "You know what that means."

Michael opened his mouth then closed it.

"I saw empty bottles in the dumpster," Izzy whispered.

She flinched when Michael punched the nearest feed sack.

CHAPTER 2

The sun slipped below the edge of the town with smudges of red, orange, purple. Darkness swallowed more color with each tick of the clock. It pushed families inside to escape the cold and what might be hidden in the shadows.

Behind closed doors.

Worlds narrowed.

Behind closed doors.

Belonging, sometimes mingled with dread.

Behind the Dunn family's door, the scent of cooking onions floated through the trailer house. It seeped under Izzy's bedroom door during an exciting part of her book.

Potato soup. Thick and cheesy—one of Dad's favorites—hers too.

Mom only fixed it when Dad was...mad.

They'd had it twice in the last week.

"Don't think about it." Izzy read the same page twice, then slammed the book shut, not even pressing a bookmark between the pages.

Outside a crust formed on the snow in the plummeting temperatures. Izzy scrubbed the fog from the window and watched Dad kick the truck door shut. His boots crunched through pools of light from the trailer's windows.

From the kitchen, a spoon rapped on the edge of the pan. The trailer vibrated when Dad stumbled through the door.

"Supper," Mom called.

Everyone gathered like condemned prisoners.

Behind closed doors in their spots around the table.

Only sounds—ice clinking in glasses, Mom's nervous throat clearing.

Izzy's eyes darted from Mom to Michael and Beth to her dad. His jaw clenched. Everyone swallowed their breath, waiting for him to release whatever was stewing in him like soup on the stove, on the verge of burning.

Izzy ached for a book—words on a page that would take her somewhere else.

No. Way.

Bringing a book to supper would only make things worse. Once, when she rode with Dad on a feed delivery, he grabbed a book she'd borrowed from Ariel.

"Quit that damn reading!" he'd hollered. He slammed it behind the truck seat, and the pages ripped when he threw it.

Just thinking about it made her sick.

Nope, reading during supper would tick him off even more. Instead, Izzy thought about how she'd sort of promised her friends to ask Mom about her birthday.

Nothing Izzy tried to imagine came anywhere close to the skating party Jody had. She had a list of ideas in her sunflower spiral, but she had to convince her mom and dad that a twelfth birthday was a big deal.

Hoping to be brave enough to ask tonight.

But then, there was the soup.

And Mom's answer to Beth about the math thing.

And the whiskey in the glass beside Dad's bowl.

"Mom, track tryouts are in a couple weeks," Michael said.

Izzy stretched her leg in search of his foot. Not a good time, she thought.

Dad stopped chewing. His eyes hard on Michael. "What's that got to do with you?"

Michael squirmed in his seat and glanced at Mom.

A slight shake of her head, and she stood. "Jim, you want some more soup?" She took his bowl to the stove.

"Well...I've been practicing, and I have some money saved. But..."

Dad slammed his glass on the table. The whiskey splattered on Izzy's arm.

"But, nothing! Plenty of running to do at the store."

Michael shrank in his chair.

Dad took another drink. "Quit trying to be something you're not." He rubbed his hand over his mouth. "You're never gonna be any more than you are right now."

Izzy held her breath while she watched Michael. A vein pulsed on his forehead. His thumb pulverized a cracker on his plate.

Beside him, Beth was a statue, barely breathing.

Mom set Dad's soup bowl on the table, then took Michael's to fill it. She squeezed his shoulder when Dad wasn't looking.

Why didn't she stand up to Dad? Tell him how fast Michael was. Izzy wanted enough courage to tell him herself, but that wasn't how this game was played.

Keep your thoughts to yourself—don't make things worse.

Beth was a pro at it. She knew how to be invisible, unmoving. Izzy counted the seconds between her sister's blinks—thirty-eight, thirty-nine...

Why couldn't she and Michael be more like her? Maybe that's why Beth was Dad's favorite.

Even with all the drama, she wanted to finish the question about her birthday. Don't be dumb, she told herself. Bad timing. But, she'd have to face her friends at school.

Which would be worse? Dad or them?

Then, under the table, *tap, tap, tap*. The movement eased some of her tension.

"Ah-hem," Mom cleared her throat and pressed a hand on top of Izzy's knee.

Someone shoved a foot against her leg. She sat up straight but still squirmed. Across the table, the statue came to life and gave Izzy a, *you better stop or else* look. Michael's eyebrows scrunched in a frown, but his eyes never shifted from the pile of cracker dust he continued to crush. They knew what was coming, and everyone tried to warn her. She struggled to stop—meant to just think about the rhythm. The taps were softer but not soft enough.

"If you can't sit still, leave the table." Dad reached for Izzy's hair and yanked it.

Hard.

"Oww!" Pain spread across her scalp, making her whole body scream with the hurt. She squeezed her eyes shut and reached to touch the tender spot. Surprised there was no blood on her fingers when she looked.

Dad's bloodshot eyes locked on her. She held his stare and pressed her lips together, determined not to cry.

She felt Mom's hand on her shoulder. "Eat your soup, Izzy, before it gets cold." Her voice sounded pinched.

Was that all? Eat your soup?

Ugly words filled Izzy's mouth. Her lips puckered with them. Her face burned. Beth and Michael concentrated on their bowls like there was something important hiding under the potatoes. How could they just sit there, pretending to eat? Izzy's chair made a hollow scraping when she pushed away from the table. She knew she couldn't keep quiet like Michael and let Dad win.

So, she retreated—hating herself for being such a coward.

CHAPTER 3

I zzy pushed her arm to the back of her drawer like she did most nights. Touching a familiar coolness, she pulled out a small china dog—a gift from Dad when she was little. She crawled to the top bunk and stroked the slick finish across her upper lip. Her other hand touched the still aching spot on her head. The real hurt wasn't from the pain—not even from the embarrassment.

It came back to one thing. Always.

She hated the bully Dad became when he drank.

She hated herself even more—too scared to ask him to stop.

Clenching her teeth until they ached, she reached for the notebook hiding under her pillow. She finger-traced the sunflower on the cover. Dad used to bring Mom the gold flowers with dark centers. He called them "happy flowers."

She flipped pages, stopping to smile at Ariel's ghost cartoon, then flipped a few more until she found what she needed—*Family Rules.*

Twenty rules that were almost impossible to keep. Her throat ached with pinched back tears. She gripped the pen until her hand trembled.

#21 Don't tap your feet at supper

#22 Don't expect any help from Beth, Michael, or Mom

She heard loud voices through the walls. Pressed the pen even harder, cutting into the paper.

#23 Dad thinks he wins.

She stared at the china dog in her hand and remembered the father who used to care about her. There had been a chair by a window. Dad had gathered her onto his lap, and they rocked back and forth. The smell of his skin was spicy from his aftershave. She had pressed her ear to his chest. His heart thumped with a steady drumlike beat. It made her feel safe and warm as he told the story.

"Once upon a time, there was a little white dog with bright eyes."

Izzy had pulled her thumb from her mouth. "What happened to the doggie?"

"Well, he wanted to go with his brother and sister, but he was too small." Scooting Izzy off his lap, Dad had reached to a high shelf. "Close your eyes and hold out your hand, little Isabel." She'd felt something cool and smooth. "Now, open your eyes." It was a small china dog with painted eyes and a pink tongue.

"Is it mine?" she asked.

"If you can take good care of it."

She remembered kissing Dad's whiskery cheek. The china dog with bright eyes became her favorite thing in her world.

More angry voices from the kitchen interrupted her remembering. She rubbed the cool surface of the dog against her lip again and wondered where that daddy had gone.

The one that told stories.

The one that smiled and brought Mom the happy flowers.

The one that never pulled her hair.

She changed into her nightgown, turned out the light, and settled under the covers. The door slid open and then bumped shut. Izzy peeked through eye slits at Beth staring out the window. Her body was a silhouette against silver moonlight. Beth turned, and Izzy squeezed her eyes tight.

"You awake?" Beth whispered.

Izzy moaned and rolled away from words she knew were coming.

"You should've stopped." A drawer scraped open. "Mom said not to bother him. Michael wouldn't let it go either."

Good for him, Izzy thought.

A sigh from Beth.

A long silence.

A soft snoring from the lower bunk.

Izzy rolled to her back and stared at the ceiling, so close she could touch it. She ran her fingers over the rough surface and picked at a small hole next to the wall. She wondered, for the umpteenth time, why she couldn't be more like Beth.

The silent statue.

The favorite daughter.

But Izzy knew. She didn't want to be silent. She wanted to scream.

****

While the town slept, the eleven o'clock train sliced through the dark. It moved like a rumbling shadow, eating up tracks and sending its lonesome wale through the chill.

Izzy lay awake, counting the seconds until the next horn blast. One...two...three... One long whistle sounded as the train approached a crossing. It was a sad and empty sound. A sound that made her wish she hadn't pretended to be asleep when Beth wanted to talk. She leaned over the edge of the bed and touched her sister's foot under the blanket.

"Beth. Beth, you awake?"

"What do you want?" Beth mumbled.

"Did you hear the train whistle?" Izzy propped her chin on her palm and leaned into her elbow. "Why is it such a sad sound?"

Beth groaned. "You think too much. Go to sleep."

Izzy dropped back onto her bed and squeezed her head, hoping to slow down her brain. One touch of the tender spot and instead of train whistles, she replayed supper, and the tapping, and the hair-pulling.

What if Michael hadn't interrupted her? What if she'd gotten her courage and asked about her birthday sleepover? She imagined her mom and dad smiling at one another with an unspoken knowing that their little girl was growing up fast. Mom would have asked what kind of cake she wanted. She and Dad would have said chocolate at the same time—his favorite, hers too.

Izzy smiled and reached for several strands of hair. Her fingers twisted it into a silky knot that relaxed her—until her fingers once again grazed the tender place. The comfort and the *smiling family* fairy-tale evaporated. She slipped her hand under her pillow and touched the hidden flashlight. Beside it was the book she had longed for at supper. She flipped the switch. A faint circle of light filled the page, then a blink and nothing.

"Perfect!" she whispered.

Book in one hand, china dog in the other, she slid down the bunk and tiptoed into the hall. The floor popped under her weight, causing her to stop and listen to Michael snoring and the train at another crossing. The furnace clicked, blowing out warm air. At the bathroom, she slid the door shut, and let out the breath she'd been holding. There was a soft glow from the nightlight over the sink. She opened the book. Too dark. Scanning the room, she saw the vanilla candle on the back of the stool. Izzy shrugged, then set the china dog on the cabinet. She reached for a box of matches in the medicine cabinet and caught a brown bottle before it tumbled out. She lit the wick.

Standing between the flickering candle and the glow of the nightlight, the words were clearer. Soon, she was lost in the excitement of teenage spies in secret passages. The enemy, so close, the heroine could smell the bad guy's sweat.

Her eyes couldn't scan the words fast enough.

She didn't hear the footsteps.

Didn't remember the candle when the bathroom door slid open. Hot wax burned her fingers when she caught the tipped jar. The flame sputtered then fired up after she set the jar on the cabinet.

"What do you think you're doing fillin' your head with that crap again?" Dad's words were even more garbled than before. "Get back to bed!" The candlelight made surreal shadows on his face.

Izzy's heart pounded in her ears. She slipped under his arm and ran to her room. On her bed, she waited for the slamming against her ribs to stop.

Wondered how the rest of the family could sleep.

Questioned what she'd done that was so bad.

"If you hate us so much," she whispered, "why don't you just leave?" She covered her head with her arms, shocked that she'd said the words out loud.

The furnace gently hummed.
Her pulse slowed—eyes fluttered.
Final thought, before sleep.
A flickering candle.
On the cabinet's edge.

CHAPTER 4

Frost sparkled on every surface. A dog barked, chimes from the church on the hill echoed, and Taggert Creek was bathed in the glow of frozen moonlight.

So beautiful.

So peaceful.

So deceptive.

BEEP! BEEP! BEEP!

An ear-piercing alarm bounced off the walls of the Dunn's trailer house, shattering the stillness. Izzy fell from her bed and landed on her sister, crouching on the floor.

"Beth! What is it?"

"Fire. Stay down." Beth coughed. "Stay low." The sisters crawled from their room. They bumped into Michael in the hall.

"Gotta get out," he called as he led them through the smoke. "Crawl!"

Izzy stopped when she remembered her notebook and china dog still in her bed or maybe on the floor when she fell. She turned to go back but heard a low roar. Above her, a gray monster of smoke churned like a storm.

"Mom, Dad?" she called.

"Front door!" Mom shouted. "We'll go out the back."

"Izzy!" Michael yelled. "Come on!"

Izzy crawled as far as she could toward Michael's voice. Her legs trembled, and her lungs burned. "I can't," she said. "Maybe, put my head down, just a minute."

Crash!

Exploding pieces rained down on her. Her fuzzy brain told her she had to move.

Michael grunted as he kicked the door, and it smacked against the side of the trailer. The fire roared, sucking in air.

"Go! Now!" Michael pushed Beth in front of him.

Izzy felt her brother's hands shove her through the door, and then she was rolling on the frozen ground. She crawled away from the concrete porch, coughing and whimpering.

Mom shouted from the back door, "Get up! Run! Get away from the trailer." She ran to them sobbing, wrapping them in her arms—a momma bird protecting her babies.

"Where's Dad?" Michael's voice squeaked. Izzy held her breath. Mom turned in all directions, eyes frantic.

Sirens.

Flashing lights.

Shouts.

"Did everyone get out?" Tom Norton, Taggert Creek's fire chief, asked. "Vicky, where's Jim? Was he home with you?"

A shiver rattled through Izzy.

"Jim? Jim!" Mom stepped toward the trailer then turned back to stare at the kids.

"Daddy!" Beth screamed.

Mr. Norton stepped in front of Mom. "Vicki, stay here with the kids." He pulled a radio from a flap on his coat. "Jim's still in the trailer." His breath puffed into the cold air. "Get some blankets for these kids, and someone take them to my car."

Mom choked and said, "I found him in the hall when the smoke alarm went off."

Izzy stared at her mom's face in the light of the flames. Black smoke and ash outlined her nose and upper lip.

"I thought he was right behind me!" Mom said.

Smoke rolled from the edge of the trailer's roof like it was alive. The fire roared even louder, and the firemen shouted orders to one another. Izzy covered her ears. She stared at the glowing embers catching in the cold breeze, floating away like fireflies. So pretty.

She startled when something exploded inside the trailer. Michael pulled Beth and her close to his chest. It felt strange to have him do something so tender, so loving. Some of the terror seeped from her. But even that was ripped away when the memory of her own words shouted in her head.

If you hate us so much, why don't you just leave?

She pulled away and shook even harder. She sensed someone close and felt the weight of a blanket across her shoulders. Beside her, an old woman with wild hair touched Izzy's cheek with her icy fingers, and then she was gone.

"Did you see that lady?" Izzy asked Beth, but her sister was silent. Her face a black and white picture.

A voice shouted from the crowd that had come to watch. "You keep that fire away from my trailer!" their neighbor hollered.

"We're doing our best, Mr. Pardee," Tom Norton said, "but let's get your car moved just in case."

Like a line of zombies, Izzy and her family followed the police officer through the crowd to Tom Norton's car.

"Here you go," the officer said. "The heater's running full blast." He tucked Mom into the front, then opened the back door for Izzy, Beth, and Michael. "You'll get warmed up in a bit." Someone handed him a steaming Styrofoam cup. "Drink this, Vicky. Everybody just wait here." And then he was gone.

Wait?

Wait for what?

Izzy looked at Beth in the middle seat and Michael next to the window. Beth was using the edge of her nightgown to wipe smoke and tears from her face. Her perfect nails, broken and bleeding. Michael's coughing shook the car.

From the back-seat window, Izzy watched smoke billowing into the dark sky. It blocked the moon. Silver light, now murky and grotesque. How long since she watched Beth stare at that same moon from their bedroom window? How long since they jumped from the porch? Since the strange woman dropped the blanket around Izzy's shoulders.

The hissing air from the heater's vents blocked sounds outside the car. Breath fogged the windows until, beyond their cocoon, the family could only see shadows and a muted red glow.

Izzy was tempted to crawl into the front seat. Her mother would stroke her hair like she did when other bad dreams came. But this was too real to be a dream, and her mother was a stranger with a steaming cup trembling in her hand.

The car's front door opened, and Tom Norton brought in cold and more smoke. He rested his hands on the steering wheel, then turned his body in the seat to look at Mom.

"Vicky, I've got tough news." He glanced to the backseat. "Maybe we should step outside." Mom nodded and reached for the door, but Michael put his hand on her shoulder.

"No, Mom. We want to know." Izzy nodded with her sister when Michael looked at them, but part of her wanted to run and hide from the fire chief's words.

Tom Norton cleared his throat. "Okay. Here it is." He rubbed the back of his neck. "It's a total loss. It's a miracle you and the kids got out in time."

He hesitated.

"And, we found Jim." He laid his arm across the seat and touched Mom's shoulder, "He didn't make it. He's gone."

Someone gasped.

Mom made a sound like some hurt animal.

Beth whimpered.

Michael pounded on the car door over and over again.

Izzy called out, "Wait. No, he's not dead. I saw him crawling behind Mom."

Tom Norton's face was framed in the rearview mirror, pale bloodshot eyes, lips pressed in a straight line. He shook his head back and forth.

Izzy pulled the blanket over her body, curled her knees to her chest, tapped the side of her head against the cold glass. The pain distracted her from his words, from thoughts of a flickering candle on the cabinet's edge, from the weight of what she'd done.

****

The stench of smoke hung above the town like something evil. It followed the Dunn family to the motel on the highway.

Someone led them to tiny rooms where they crawled between scratchy sheets and pretended to sleep.

Someone paid their bill and brought breakfast to eat with plastic forks on paper plates.

Someone called Grandma and Grandpa Dunn in Missouri. They weren't with them, and then they were—looking smaller, somehow broken, talking only in whispers.

Izzy tried to pretend it was a routine visit where her Dad's parents brought little gifts and good things to eat. But then she saw Grandma's messy hair, not sprayed fresh from the beauty shop, and felt Grandpa's unshaven cheek scratching her face.

"Come here, Isabel," Grandma hugged her and cried tears into her hair.

Everything had changed.

Dad was dead.

Her fault.

CHAPTER 5

A cold Kansas wind herded clouds across the sky—so plump with snow you could almost taste it. The wind cleared the air of smoke but couldn't erase the sadness that lay across Taggert Creek like a grey blanket. A blue tent, open on one side, blocked some of that wind in the cemetery on the edge of town. The minister's voice floated across a mound of dirt and a huddled group of mourners.

"Even though I walk through the valley of the shadow of death, I will fear no evil for thou art with me…"

Izzy and her brother and sister should have been in school, taking a test, or hurrying to class. Mom should have been talking to customers with Dad on a feed delivery, his dog curled up beside him on the seat. Instead, they shivered in folding chairs on fake grass, with Grandma and Grandpa Dunn beside them. They faced Dad's coffin—so close Izzy could have touched it.

But she didn't.

Touching the cold metal would make the nightmare real.

She wanted to pretend it wasn't.

Everything she wore was borrowed—shoes that pinched her feet, a coat with rolled-up sleeves, and her best friend's beautiful dress. Ariel had worn it to their sixth-grade Christmas concert that seemed like forever ago instead of a few months. Beth, Michael, and Mom had borrowed clothes too. But Dad, inside the grey coffin, had *new* clothes—a jacket, a white shirt, even a tie. No one would see, but Mom wanted him to look nice.

"Don't think about it," Izzy whispered to herself and rolled the dress's pink ribbon between her fingers. She stared at the red flowers on the coffin, pulling in their scent, wishing they were sunflowers, the happy flowers. She focused on Pastor Smith's lips—his words slipping in and out of her mind.

"Bad things happen to good people. We can't change that. But we can help this young family survive the dark days ahead. Let us pray."

Izzy knew it was wrong not to bow her head, not to close her eyes, and talk to God. But she couldn't. God knew the fire was her fault. She was afraid to pray—terrified it would make her shout out the truth. Instead, she watched the wind pick up the pastor's hair revealing a bald spot. She followed the breeze as it whistled into the field beside the cemetery. A bobwhite quail sang from the tall grass. Its low notes, high notes judged her.

Your fault.

Your fault.

Your fault.

She bit her lip to keep from screaming. That's when she saw the lady—the same old lady who stood beside her the night of the fire. This time she was leaning on a broom. Alone, just outside the tent, eyes open, not praying either, reaching her gloved hand toward Izzy then pulling it back over her heart.

"Amen," said Pastor Smith.

Izzy turned to Beth and whispered, "Who is that lady with the broom?"

"What?" Beth looked at her like she was crazy. Izzy pointed at a blank spot where the lady had stood. She wanted to explain, but then the service was over. She waited with her family while people filed past them—their words like slaps.

"Such a shame."

"So sorry."

"Beautiful service."

Mrs. Bartlett, a volunteer at the library, stood off to the side and said in a loud whisper, "Poor little girl. She's lost her father. Can't be more than nine or ten."

"I'm almost twelve," Izzy whispered.

Someone handed her a drooping flower—the cold air stealing its life. She followed her family from the shelter and moved toward the line of cars that snaked over the hillside. Grandpa Dunn caught her when she tripped on the uneven ground. He tucked Mom in the front of the car, then Grandma, Beth, and Izzy in the back. Michael rode with the other men who had carried Dad.

The silence inside the car made Izzy want to scream.

"It was a nice service, wasn't it?" Grandma asked, interrupting the quiet.

Izzy just nodded, afraid to trust her words. She looked back to the mound of dirt and the dying flowers beside it. Gravel crackled and popped under the tires. The line of cars hesitated at the cemetery gate then inched forward.

Izzy ached to go home, to feel normal. To climb onto her top bunk and hear the scratching of a felt-tipped pen on a clean white page. Even having her dad yell at her would be better than this. They drove past the black trailer shell. She turned her head from it and almost choked on the smoke she was sure filtered through the vents in the car's heater.

A long line followed them through town and past the feed store. Izzy pictured Dad's dog, Maverick, curled up on his blankets. She wiped the fog from the side window, and her breath caught. The woman with the broom stood in front of the old theater next to the feed store. White hair blowing in the wind, gloved hand reaching toward the car. Izzy turned in the seat to look out the back window.

"How could it be the same lady?" she mumbled. "Did you see her?" she asked a little louder. No one answered. A shiver ran up her neck and down her arms. She dropped to the seat and leaned into Grandma Dunn.

The line of cars turned right on Main Street. People of the town stopped where they were, in front of the cafe on the corner, outside the post office with its wind-whipped flag, and beside their cars in front of the drug store. All the way to the church on the highway, people moved their cars to the side to let them pass—hats off, heads bowed.

"Grandma, why are they doing that?" Izzy asked.

Grandma lifted her glasses to wipe her eyes. "It's a sign of respect, darling. They're remembering the ones they've lost and showing us they understand."

Warmth stirred in Izzy's chest for a few seconds. Then, she remembered. Those people couldn't understand the guilt she felt. None of them caused their father to die. She bit into her lip and tasted blood.

****

Izzy heard Mom talking, whispering to Grandma and Grandpa around a table at the motel that night. Mom's voice was brittle, like it could shatter without warning.

"We needed some extra money. Jim said we could let the trailer's insurance go for a little while—just until we got caught up with our bills." A sob choked her words. "He wanted," she hesitated, "he wanted to drop his life insurance too, but we didn't. What would we do if I hadn't made him keep it?" She blew her nose. "It's just barely enough to cover the funeral."

Izzy took a breath to tell Mom the truth about the burning candle.

Stopped herself before the words came tumbling out.

She ran her tongue over a ragged place from chewing the inside of her cheek.

Grandpa cleared his throat. "Vicky," he tapped a pencil on the flimsy table, "you and the kids come live with us."

No, Izzy thought. I can't leave Ariel and Jody. And what about Dad's dog? Grandma would never let them keep Maverick in the house. She'd make him stay outside, and he'd always slept in the feed store—guarding it. Izzy pressed her teeth down until her jaws ached.

"It'll be crowded, but we can make do." Grandpa scooted forward in his chair. "What do you think?" Izzy held her breath and strained to hear Mom's words.

"Thank you, but no. I won't take the kids away from their friends." Mom's voice moved closer. "Not now." The bed sagged when she sat beside Izzy and stroked her hair with gentle fingers. Her touch felt nice, safe. Izzy let go of the breath she'd trapped in her lungs.

"There's a way we can stay in Taggert Creek." Mom stood and walked back to the table. "I'm keeping the feed store. We'll live in the back rooms."

Izzy sat straight up and shouted, "No!"

Beth moved in slow motion beside her.

"Oh, Vicky. You can't do that," Grandma said.

Grandpa stood and bumped his head on the hanging light. He grabbed the shade with both hands to stop the swaying. "Vicky, we won't be telling you what to do, but you've got to think this thing through. I understand you wanting to keep the store," his voice shook. "It was Jimmy's dream." He stood and pulled the orange drapes open, "But live there…?" His voice bounced off the glass. He turned back to Mom. "Jimmy wouldn't want that."

Izzy flinched when mom's fist came down hard on the table.

"Well, Jimmy's not here!" Mom shouted. "It's not what I want either."

Beth's icy fingers squeezed Izzy's hand.

A picture of the feed store's back rooms popped into Izzy's mind.

Bare bulbs swinging.

Dark, damp walls.

Mice hiding behind boxes.

Izzy shivered and pulled the pillow over her head. It wasn't enough to block out Mom's words.

"We'll make it work," Mom whispered.

"It's all we've got."

CHAPTER 6

Sunlight burned through winter skies over Kansas. It gave a warmth and glow that brought the people of Taggert Creek out of their sadness and back to normal.

Normal for everyone except the Dunn family.

Their upside-down world was a nightmare that wouldn't stop.

Next to nothing was left to carry in cardboard boxes to the back rooms of the feed store. The move wasn't like in the past. Dad's plans to make better money always meant a different place to live. This move was different.

Izzy waited with Grandma, Beth, and Michael at the motel while volunteers from the church scrubbed and painted the storage rooms. Mom hadn't wanted them to see it until it was fixed up.

Izzy imagined mice and bugs crawling across wet paint, making tracks on the concrete floor.

"Maybe this is my punishment," she spoke to her reflection in the motel mirror. She picked up a comb. It snapped when she pulled it through her tangled hair. She stared at the pieces in her hand, feeling just as jagged. Living with mice and roaches sounded bad, but she knew it wasn't enough to make up for what she'd done.

She moved from the bathroom to the large window facing the school on the next hill. The glass felt cool on her forehead as she pressed it there. She watched kids run from the school to the waiting cars like scattering ants.

An odd disappointment wormed through her.

Sadness that she wasn't carrying tons of homework.

Loss that she wasn't complaining about last hour dragging on and on.

Izzy jumped when the phone rang from the table between the beds. Grandma shut off the soccer game Michael had been watching. He stood, saying nothing.

"Hello," Beth said into the mouthpiece. "Okay, Mom." Beth glanced at Izzy. "Yes, we're excited to see what you've done. Do you want to talk to Grandma? Okay, we'll leave now. Bye."

Michael grabbed his coat and slammed the room's door as he left.

"Get your things, girls." Grandma said. "Your mother's waiting."

All the way to the feed store, Grandma's *be positive* words buzzed in Izzy's head. She ached for a book to block them. Instead, she counted telephone poles and stared at fields of dried cornstalk bones.

The car pulled into a space across from the store office. Mom waved from the doorway, then emptied a large trashcan. The sound of shattering liquor bottles hit the metal sides of the dumpster.

Izzy's stomach twisted. She hugged her knees to her chest.

Grandma cleared her throat and looked over her glasses at Beth and Izzy in the backseat, then Michael beside her.

"Remember what we talked about. No complaining,"

Izzy wondered why grownups always said things like, "we talked about" when it was really just them telling.

"Michael?" Grandma asked.

He raised his head. "Sure. We'll pretend everything's wonderful." Grandma ignored his attitude and turned to the backseat. "Girls?"

Izzy nodded when Beth did, but she wanted to agree with Michael's sarcasm.

"Okay, let's go."

Beth and Michael followed Grandma into the office. Izzy ran straight to Maverick, where he fought a chain near the building's foundation.

"What's the matter, boy?"

The dog whined, then dropped to his belly, smearing slobber on Izzy's coat sleeve. She looked at Maverick's one brown eye and one blue.

"Are you missing him?" He licked her cheek. Why didn't *she* miss him? She buried her face in the dog's fur. "I'm sorry, Maverick. I said I wished he'd go away, but I didn't mean it."

Thump, thump, thump.

Izzy stood and looked toward the theater's roof next door. Backing from the building, she shaded her eyes. Pigeons slipped in and out the vents on top.

Thump, thump, thump.

The hair on Izzy's arms prickled. Glancing at the office building on the right to see if Mom was watching—hoping she was—Izzy fought her urge to look through the cracks in the plywood-covered windows.

"Quit being such a baby," she whispered and walked to the front of the theater.

She peeked through the boarded-up glass door.

Something moved in the shadows. Izzy jumped when Maverick pushed his wet nose against her hand.

"Izzy, where are you?" Mom hollered from the office doorway.

Izzy slipped into the alley by the theater before Mom noticed. She tried to steady her voice. "Be right there. Just checking on Maverick."

Mom walked toward her, rubbing her arms. "He's fine. Don't you want to see what we've done?" Mom hurried back to the store without an answer.

"Not really," Izzy muttered.

Thump, thump, thump. A shiver traveled up her back. A movement, a stirring at the other end of the alley, stole her attention from the sound.

"Izzy!" Beth shouted from the office door. "Mom won't show us anything until you get in here. Hurry up!"

"Be right there," Izzy said. She backed from the alley, then turned and ran to the office.

The sense of being watched followed.

CHAPTER 7

Izzy trailed behind Beth and Michael into the back room. Bare bulbs still swung from the ceiling, making pools of light, but a new wood and paint smell mixed with old mustiness. Even though it was cleaner, Izzy was two sniffs from a sneeze.

"Here's the bathroom," Mom said. "The Weisner family from the hardware store put in a shower where that floor drain was. Wasn't that nice?" She was trying too hard—just like Dad did the day he showed them the trailer house he bought. The one that now lay twisted and black.

Grandma's hand on her back guided her into the one-person-sized bathroom. There was a new coat of tan paint on the concrete blocks. Someone had hung a picture of a black and white cow on the wall.

"Well, isn't that pretty?" Grandpa said. His words sounded happy, but his eyes were sad.

"And here's the kitchen." Mom waved her arm toward the old metal sink in the corner. Someone had scraped off the crud and attached a metal shelf to the side.

"See, we have cabinets and everything," she said as she pulled the rough plywood doors toward her. She slammed them shut when a cockroach skittered on the edge. "And, over here are our bedrooms.

Mine is on the left, yours in the center, Michael, and you girls on the right." They all stood staring at what looked like a huge plywood box with three openings.

Grandpa gave Michael a little shove, "Aren't you going inside?"

Michael glanced back at Izzy and Beth, then disappeared into the center opening.

"Go on, girls," Grandma whispered.

Izzy followed Beth into what was more like a closet than a room. The only light came from a tiny window next to the ceiling and a single lamp perched on an overturned box. Most of the space was filled with a metal bunk bed. A funky smell made Izzy cover her nose and pray it wasn't coming from the mattresses.

Mom continued her tour from the doorway since there really wasn't room for another body in the space. "One of your dad's friends built the walls," she said. "Sorry they don't go all the way to the ceiling, but they'll give us a little privacy."

Michael and Grandpa's voices floated over the top of the wall.

Mom's eyes darted up. "Maybe we can find some paint on sale later," she said, "to brighten things up a little."

Mom turned to look at them. Izzy sighed and searched for something positive to say.

Beth said, "It's nice, Mom."

Nice! Really?

It reminded Izzy of an underground bunker she saw in a film at school—good if a tornado was roaring overhead, but not the kind of place you want to sleep for the rest of your life.

Izzy scanned the room and watched another cockroach run up the wall. Of all the old rental houses they'd lived in, this was the worst. She kept waiting for the question her mom always asked when they moved into a new place—*Where should we put the Christmas tree?* But Mom just talked on and on about plastic tubs for their clothes and how homey things were going to be.

Finally the three adults headed to the office. Izzy stood staring at the bug while Beth dug through a plastic bag filled with toothpaste and deodorant.

"Have you seen a brush or comb?" Beth asked.

Izzy didn't answer but handed her a thick-toothed comb she spotted in one of the bags. She watched Beth comb her dark hair in the distorted mirror hanging by a wire. Izzy pulled a handful of her own hair in front of her eyes. She twisted the limp strands between her fingers. "This place is really horrible, isn't it Beth?"

Beth just nodded while she pulled loose hairs from the comb.

"We're leaving, girls," Grandpa hollered from the office.

Izzy and Beth pushed through the swinging door to where their grandparents were putting on their coats.

"I want to stay with you at the motel tonight," Izzy said as she wrapped her arms around Grandma's neck.

"No!" Mom's loud voice caused Izzy to jump back. "Sorry," Mom said. "I didn't mean to yell. I just think we need to spend this first night in our new home together." Mom rubbed Izzy's back. "Besides, they're leaving early to go back to Missouri."

"Sorry, Kiddo," Grandpa said. "We'll be back."

"Why don't you and Beth start making the beds?" Mom said.

Knowing her mom wasn't going to budge, Izzy gave her grandparents hugs, then went to her room. Beth came back a few minutes later, and they both dug through donation boxes. Izzy found a faded, pink set of sheets.

"Here, Beth, you take these."

"Thanks," Beth said but wore a blank expression and was silent while they worked. Izzy longed for some kind of normal. She needed her sister to complain about how messy she was. She stepped on the edge of Beth's mattress, but there was no reaction.

"Beth, what do you think caused the fire?" Izzy heard the words, but it was like they came from someone else's mouth.

Beth shrugged and said, "It wouldn't change anything if we knew."

For a second, Izzy was tempted to tell about the candle. Maybe Beth could tell her what to do.

No.

She could never tell her sister.

Or anyone else.

CHAPTER 8

Paper plates from a microwave supper went in the trash, and Mom began unloading boxes of donated kitchen stuff. "You kids get busy on your homework."

"Mom, we don't have…," Izzy started to say, but Beth grabbed her arm and shook her head. Izzy followed her sister to their room and listened to Michael slam things against the thin wall. Beth sat on the bottom bunk flipping the pages of an old math book someone gave them.

"How can you just read math for fun?" Izzy asked. Beth shrugged and turned the page. "Not me. Give me a mystery over math anytime." She studied Beth's face for a reaction.

Nothing.

She grabbed a book from the box Mom said Ariel's dad brought that morning. Without warning, she felt uneasy. She tried to ignore it and climbed to the top bunk, ready to escape. Dropping her head on the pillow, she waited for the safe feeling of her own bed. The feeling didn't come.

Maybe it was the new pillow Grandma bought.

Or the disgusting smell from the mattress.

Or the exposed feeling the short wall gave her.

Beth was below her, sighing, but Izzy felt alone in the dim light that didn't quite reach the pages of her book.

Out of habit, she slipped her hand under her pillow, expecting to touch the cool metal of her flashlight. For a second, she was confused. It wouldn't matter anyway, she thought. The batteries had lost their juice. That's why she went to the bathroom that night. That's why she lit the candle.

Her stomach lurched. Her throat went tight like someone had wrapped their fingers around her neck and squeezed. She could swear the dark ceiling above was sinking, smothering her. She slid over the edge of the bed and peeked at her sister lying on her back. Beth's eyes were closed with the math book across her chest. Izzy stumbled to the kitchen, trying to breathe in a normal way, so Mom wouldn't ask questions. Wouldn't worry.

"Mom," she struggled to form the words, "can I read in the office? It's too dark on my bed."

Mom sighed. "I guess it'll be okay." Izzy pretended not to notice her mother's hand brush against her cheeks.

"I'm turning in early," Mom said. "Don't stay up too late. Oh, and do you feel okay taking Maverick out before you go to bed?"

"Sure," Izzy said, then wished she hadn't said it.

It was strange to be in the store so late at night—strange to see moonlight through the windows instead of sunshine. Maverick looked up from where he lay curled on an old blanket. Every night, before bed, Dad had gone back to the store just to take Maverick for a walk. That ugly dog was one of the few things that made him smile. His loyalty to Maverick had started on a feed delivery to the animal shelter. Izzy had gone with him and saw her dad petting and talking to the strange-looking dog.

A lady with a bucket and shovel whispered to Izzy, "Your dad has the right touch. Maverick doesn't take to people easily."

Neither did Dad. Izzy knew they needed each other. A plan came together when Maverick was delivered to their trailer on Christmas morning with a bow around his neck and a note from Santa.

Izzy tried to remember the sound of her dad's voice when he read the note out loud.

Jim,

Maverick needs a friend, and so do you. He can ride with you in the truck and guard the feed store at night. Just let him be, and he'll come around.

Merry Christmas, from Santa and Helpers

Dad didn't look at any of them that day outside the trailer. He turned to the dog and said, "Let's go, Maverick. You look like you need a walk in the snow."

The only sound was a whine from Maverick and Dad's boots crunching through the crust on the snow. Mom herded everyone back inside. But Izzy remembered running to the driveway at the end of the trailer. She watched her dad walk, head down, hands shoved into his pockets. Maverick trotting beside him, taking uncertain looks at Dad's face. When they came to the spot where tree roots pushed up the sidewalk, Dad had stopped. He kneeled to smooth his hand along Maverick's broad back. The air was so still that morning, she could hear his deep laugh when Maverick licked his cheek.

"You are one ugly dog," Dad had said, then Maverick put his paw on his knee. Dad turned and looked up. His eyes crinkled with a half-smile, and Izzy had felt like crying and laughing at the same time.

Standing in the middle of the office, with moonlight peeking through the blinds, she closed her eyes and tried to press that good day memory deep.

Maybe taking care of Maverick would make up for the candle. The dog's collar jingled as if he could hear her thoughts. She walked to where he stretched his long legs. "Hey Maverick, how you doing?" A soft moan rumbled deep inside him when she rubbed his ears. He allowed it for a bit, then turned in circles to find his sleeping spot.

"Okay, boy. You snooze while I read." She walked to Mom's desk and turned on the lamp. Izzy fanned the pages of the book—pulling in the scent of paper and ink. She couldn't wait to open to the first words, to escape into someone else's life.

But she stopped.

Watching out for Maverick wouldn't be enough. Dad's last words flew into her mind.

"What you think you're doing fillin' your head with that crap again?"

Izzy scanned the first page. The words all blurred together, and she forced herself to slam the book shut. Maybe she didn't deserve something she loved this much.

It could be her punishment.

For the candle.

For the fire.

For wishing he would go away.

One last touch of the cover and she hid the book in the trash under some papers. The smell of a rotting apple in the trash made her stomach churn. She grabbed Dad's coat from the hook where she'd left it the day of the fire. Pulling in his scent, still strong in the fabric, she wrapped it around her body.

"Let's go, Maverick." The dog wiggled his stub tail and unfolded his legs. Clipping the leash with a snap, Izzy stood and opened the office door. She forced herself to think about dogs barking in the distance, about the silhouettes the bare trees made against the night sky. About anything except the book buried next to a rotting apple. She pulled the door shut before she could change her mind.

The moon slipped behind the clouds, making it dark outside the pool of light from the store's lit sign. The air was clean and cold. It allowed her to breathe deeper than she had since walking into the storage rooms that afternoon.

"I don't know if I can stand this place without my books," she whispered to no one.

A low growling rumbled in the dog's chest. A shadow moved at the edge of the alley.

"Don't even think about it, Maverick," Izzy said.

He ignored her words and towed her into the area between the feed storage building and the old theater.

She fought panic over who or what could be hiding in the dark. At the other end of the alley, two eyes glowed next to the old car that had permanently rusted to its spot.

"Woof, woof!" Maverick's bark echoed off the brick canyon. A cat streaked around the corner, and the dog followed.

"Maverick! Stop!" Izzy hissed. He dragged her to the back of the theater, where the cat slipped around the old car and into a hole in the bricks beside the back door. Maverick slid to a stop. He gave Izzy a satisfied look, his tongue hanging from the side of his mouth.

"What are you so happy about, you old ugly dog? You didn't catch that cat." She rubbed his ears. "Hurry up and get your business done. This place is creepy." Maverick ignored her again and sniffed through the crack of the barely open door.

Open door?

Mom always said to stay away, but Izzy and her friends tried the door every time they cut through the alley. Izzy was curious, but on those forbidden attempts, when the door wouldn't budge, she had to *pretend* disappointment with Ariel and Jody.

She didn't have to pretend now. She could pull Maverick back to the feed store, and no one would know how her legs turned to jelly at the thought of going into the old building.

So, why was she a statue?

Outside a possibly haunted building?

Reaching for the doorknob?

Izzy pushed. The door scraped on the bottom, but it was opening. She stopped when a song floated through the musty air from inside the building.

"What'll I do, hmmm, hmmm. And I'm so blue, hmmm, hmmm, hmmm."

"Maverick?" Izzy whispered. She felt the dog's muscles stiffen. His eyes remained fixed on the half-open door.

Izzy told herself to run, but her hand froze on the knob. She held her breath, straining to hear the melody. There was beautiful loneliness in the notes that made her want to throw open the door and be swallowed up by the old building.

Thump, thump, thump. She jumped back and felt prickles run up her back and down her arms. The thumping and humming moved closer.

Run! she thought, but her feet wouldn't move.

The music stopped.

Maverick whined.

"Come, Cleopatra," a wrinkled voice said. "Let the girl and her dog be. She'll visit us soon.

Very soon."

Izzy sprinted down the alley.

For once, Maverick followed her.

CHAPTER 9

"I like that song you're humming." Mom said. "What is it?"

Izzy stopped drying the cereal bowl Mom had handed her. The soapy water gurgled in the sink drain when Mom pulled the stopper.

"I don't know," Izzy said. "Guess I heard it somewhere."

She'd heard it all right.

Last night behind the old theater.

In the dark.

Izzy didn't even realize she'd been humming out loud.

"I'm probably going crazy," she muttered.

"What'd you say?" Mom asked.

"Nothing." Izzy put the bowl on the shelf and sighed. She took the few steps toward her room, intending to write some things in her notebook. A picture of the sunflower on the cover turning black in the flames flashed across her thoughts.

"Do we have some paper I can use?" Izzy asked her mom.

Mom rubbed the back of her neck, and her eyebrows scrunched. "I guess your school paper's gone," she said. "Okay. Get some from the printer in the office."

Izzy pushed through the swinging door.

"Just a couple sheets," Mom hollered from the back room. "That paper's expensive."

Maverick stirred from his nap, and Izzy caught a whiff of wet dog from his walk earlier. She bent to rub his head. He sighed and resettled in his spot. She counted out two sheets of paper from the printer tray on Mom's desk and pulled a nice fat pen from the chipped cup beside the phone. Settling into the chair, she wrote:

The Old Theater

Supposed to be empty—not true.

Unlocked back door last night.

Someone is making thumping noises.

That "someone" may be who was singing.

That "someone" has a cat.

That "someone" may be a ghost.

Izzy's brain felt less jumbled, but number six gave her the creeps. She stared at the words then drew a picture of the theater at the bottom of the list. She laced her fingers over the top of her head and rested her elbows on the desk. The office phone rang, and she jumped.

"Izzy, will you get that?" Mom hollered from the back.

"Okay." Izzy grabbed the store phone. "Dunn's Feed."

"Hey, Izz. It's me, Ariel."

The swinging door from the back squeaked. "I'll take it now," Mom said.

"It's Ariel, but can I call her back on Dad's—on the cell phone?" Izzy bit her lip—glad Michael found the phone on the seat of the feed truck after the fire but feeling unsettled about using it.

"Sure. Just don't run down the charge." Mom handed her the cell.

"Ariel, I'll call you right back." She pushed the off button on the office phone.

Trotting to the back, she climbed to her top bunk, thankful Beth had gone to the store for Mom. She punched in the numbers, then settled on her pillow.

"Hey," Ariel said. "I've wanted to call you. Mom said to wait."

Izzy tried to answer—to say she was fine, but her throat squeezed around the words.

"I'm sorry, Izz. I bet it's really hard?"

"The worst," Izzy whispered.

It was tempting to say more. It would be such a relief to spill everything—to have someone else share her awful secret. She opened her mouth but pushed the temptation away. "I can't talk about it now, Ariel, maybe some time." She cleared her throat. "But I do have something to tell you that you won't believe."

"Is it about your birthday?" Ariel asked, then stopped.

Izzy could hear the smile disappear from Ariel's face.

"I'm sorry, Izz. I forgot about..."

"No, just listen. I took Maverick for a walk before bed last night."

"Oh, well, that's nice. You like Maverick," Ariel said.

"That's not the good part. There was this grey cat Maverick went after, and we ended up at the back door of the theater—you know the one that is always locked?"

"Sure, but how did you get so brave in the dark?" Ariel asked.

Izzy ignored Ariel's comment and whispered, "The door was unlocked, Ariel. It was open."

"What...? Wow!"

"That's not all. There was a woman. She was humming this spooky song."

"Who was it?" asked Ariel, then gasped. "I bet it was Dirty Bertie's ghost."

Izzy startled when her mom knocked on the plywood wall. "That's enough. Tell her goodbye."

"One more minute." She waited for her mom to leave. "I gotta go," she whispered. "I'll tell you more later, but Ariel...don't tell Jody. Okay?"

"Why not?" Ariel asked. "She'll be excited."

"Yeah, she will be, but please, don't tell her. You know, so it doesn't get back to my mom—yours too." The truth was, Izzy was sure Jody couldn't keep a secret like that.

"Okay," Ariel paused.

"I'll call you again when I can. Bye," Izzy punched the off button and felt a nervous twinge in her stomach. What if Ariel told Jody anyway? She tapped the phone against her forehead, then crawled from the bunk to return it to her mom.

Back on her bed, she doodled cats and flames on the printer paper beside her theater list. Supper, the night of the fire, came rushing back. She felt her cheeks burn, remembering Dad pulling her hair, knowing things would never be any better. Izzy closed her eyes and pictured the little china dog she'd carried with her when she went to the bathroom to read that night. She thought things like that were cooked in a giant oven when they were made.

Maybe it didn't burn.

Maybe it was buried in the ashes, waiting for her to find it.

The bell on the door of the office jingled.

"Good morning!" said a customer. His voice, so booming, it made Izzy cover her ears.

"Good morning," Mom said. "What can I do for you?"

"Well, now, I wasn't sure you'd be open so soon after the loss of your husband."

No way did Izzy want to stay and listen to him talk about Dad and the fire. She scribbled a note for her mom, then slipped into the office.

GOING TO THE LIBRARY

Mom nodded and kept talking to the customer. Izzy grabbed Dad's coat from the couch and stuffed the theater list into the side pocket. Her fingers touched the wrapper of a piece of coffee-flavored candy Dad loved. She shoved the candy deeper in the pocket and left the office.

The library was at the end of the block of Taggert Creek's Main Street. The alley was the fastest way—even seemed to be calling her to come, but Izzy needed time to think. She took the long way past the stores.

It was cold, but bright sunlight winked off everything, and the sky was icy blue. Izzy ran past the front of the old theater and around the corner by Belview's Gas Station. She kept her head down while walking from one store awning to the next. She counted the uneven bricks under her feet and debated with herself about looking for the china dog in the burned-out trailer. Two old men outside the bank were talking about the fire. She pulled the jacket's hood tighter over her head, but their muffled words soaked through. She ran from them, across the street, and to the library on the corner.

Izzy shivered on the curb, letting the wind bite at her face. Through the glass, she could see row after row of shelved books. The ache in her chest—that never seemed to leave—made her wince.

"That's good," she whispered to herself. Punishments are supposed to hurt. She turned and walked away from the library—not trusting herself even to go inside. Instead of going behind the laundry mat and back to the store, she went in the opposite direction. No one ever said she couldn't go back to the trailer, but there was no way Mom would say yes if she asked. She pulled the hood tighter and ran.

CHAPTER 10

Slanted winter sun sifted through naked branches and mingled with air that grew still. A male cardinal twitched on the limb of a cedar bush nearby, its bright red feathers stark against the dark green. It was a perfect winter morning in the small town.

Happy.

Peaceful.

Contented.

Unsettled by the running girl.

Izzy raced through the cold light until her lungs burned. Three blocks, that's all it was, from the library to the trailer park. Three blocks to the long strips of yellow caution tape surrounding the black skeleton. Three blocks to the nightmare she couldn't let go.

Izzy glanced beyond her shoulder, then stepped across the tape, heart pounding. Glass crunched under her feet. Cold, smoky air stung her throat.

It looked so foreign. It reminded her of a long semi-truck without the sides and roof. The melted tires hung loose on the wheels, and all that was left of the walls were pieces of black metal sticking up like bars all around the edge of the trailer floor. Strange shapes and melted globs were covered with snow and ash. Izzy reached between the trailer ribs to touch a blackened shoe.

A siren screamed in the distance, coming closer.

The terror of that night came back in a flash, and she fought to keep from screaming. She bolted around the edge of the trailer and squatted beside the remains of the trailer's wheels. Curling into a tight ball, she covered her ears from the sound, tried not to think of the candle.

Of Dad.

On the floor.

Covered in smoke.

"No, no, no!" she cried and shook her head to erase. Within seconds it was like she was deaf to all sound—except the music.

Hm, hm, hm, hmmm. Hm, hmmm.

The song she'd heard behind the theater door washed over her.

Hm, hmmm, hm-hm.

She hummed with it. Felt it vibrate in her chest.

Through her throat.

Into the air around her, evaporating the ugliness.

Izzy wanted to fly with the notes—float to the theater, follow the cat into the darkness.

A truck roared past the trailer court, pulling her back. Confused and shaking, she unfolded her body, attempted to understand what had happened. Maybe she really was going crazy. She shifted her weight to run back to the feed store.

But she couldn't.

Wouldn't leave without looking for the china dog.

She wiped her eyes with the back of her hand and scanned the remains of the trailer to find her room. She reached through the ribs with fingers that trembled so much they felt like they were on someone else's hand. Carefully sifting through ashes and melted globs, she lifted a large charred piece of wood. Her breath came in short gasps, but she kept searching until her arm began to tremble. The heavy wood slipped from her fingers and dropped. A puff of ash floated onto her face and hair.

Spitting out the dust that settled into her mouth, she backed away, intending to give up. That's when she saw the blackened stool and tub under part of the wall next to the bedroom. Light glinted off a chunky glass jar on the floor. She leaned in and reached for it. Spider web cracks covered the sides. When she raised it to her nose, she shivered. The candle wax was gone, but a faint scent of vanilla remained.

Mom's face.

Michael pushing Beth and her from the steps.

Dad crawling through the smoke.

She threw the jar at the tub and cringed when the glass shattered.

"I'm sorry!" she choked. "I didn't want you to die!" She turned to vomit in the snow.

"Hey, what are you doing here?"

Mr. Pardee from the trailer beside theirs hobbled toward her.

"I've got to go." Izzy's voice was jerky. She stumbled across the yellow tape. She needed to see her mom—to make sure she was real—not gone like Dad.

From a block away, she saw the feed store and sprinted.

Sweat under her coat.

Lungs on fire.

Taste of vomit in her mouth.

The urge to run into the alley was overwhelming. She fought it and burst through the office door.

"Boy, are you in trouble," Beth said. "You're supposed to sweep." Beth covered her nose. "Yuck! You smell gross." Then she touched Izzy's arm and whispered, "You didn't go back to the trailer, did you?"

Yanking her arm away from Beth's fingers, Izzy ran to her room. She pulled jeans and a shirt from the plastic tub in the corner. As soon as she hit the bathroom, she stripped off her clothes and stepped into the tiny fiberglass shower. The cold water took her breath, but she let the spray pelt her head and face. When the water warmed, she scrubbed away the smoke and ash.

The guilt stayed.

Like a bruise.

Black and green and ugly.

Hair still dripping, Izzy climbed to her bed and hummed the song that wouldn't leave her. How could something so beautiful make her feel safe and out of control at the same time? The air was heavy with moisture from the shower and made it even harder to pull in a full breath. She lay shivering. Counting the drips pinging into the metal sink on the other side of the plywood.

Waiting.

For what, she didn't know.

The lamp clicked on. She squinted, expecting to see Beth, but it wasn't her.

"I'm sorry, Mom. I'll go sweep now." Izzy threw her legs over the edge.

"No," Mom said. "That's not what I want to talk about." She looked over the top of her glasses. "Let's go to the kitchen."

She knows. Izzy thought.

Chief Taggert figured out what started the fire.

He told her about the…

"Isabel, I'm waiting." Mom's voice sounded more tired than mad. Izzy dropped from the top bunk and slipped into a chair beside Mom at the table.

"I know you went back to the trailer." Mom reached across the table and pushed Izzy's hair away from her face. "Mr. Pardee called." She used her fingertip to raise Izzy's chin. "Why did you do that?"

Izzy tried to speak, but fingers again were squeezing her throat. She swallowed a few times then said, "I wanted to look for...to look for something."

"Oh, honey," Mom said, "there's nothing left. Remember?"

"I know," Izzy said. Her chin trembled.

Mom reached out her arms. "Come here." And then Izzy crawled onto her lap like she had longed to the night of the fire. Mom hugged her and stroked her hair. Izzy wanted to tell her everything—about reading in the bathroom and the candle—about wishing Dad would go away. Instead, she buried her face in her mom's neck and enjoyed her touch.

Like she was something precious.

CHAPTER 11

The theater stood anchored to the earth as it had for most of a century. Gravel and broken glass crunched under foot in the narrow canyon alley shared with the feed storage building.

Back and forth, the girl counted her steps.

Back and forth, she focused on the scritch and scratch of her feet.

Back and forth, Izzy Dunn's footsteps matched the theater's thumping heartbeat.

"Nine hundred seventy-seven, nine hundred seventy-eight..."

"Isabel, where are you?" Beth shouted.

The counting stopped, and guilt rushed back. Like it had been waiting off stage.

"You don't have to yell. I'm right here," Izzy muttered.

"And, don't call me that name."

Beth peeked around the corner of the building. "What are you doing back there, ISABEL? Mom wants to talk to us."

Izzy's stomach lurched. She pulled in a shredded breath and followed her sister into the store's office.

Dust floated in the afternoon light coming through the office windows. Izzy dropped into a seat and stared at the specks. Considered counting them.

"It's time," Mom said. "It's time we quit hiding in this store. Tomorrow you go back to school." Her forehead wrinkled, her lips pressed together. "We need to get on with our lives."

Izzy watched Beth rub her finger across her thumbnail, just like Grandma. She wanted to reach for her sister's hand but held back.

Michael stood looking out the window, lost in his own thoughts. He was always looking out the window. Was he missing Dad in a good way or remembering the argument about trying out for track?

Izzy never imagined either of her parents dying, but still, she had a picture in her head of how people are supposed to act when it happens.

She was doing it all wrong.

Angry words kept looping through her thoughts.

Michael turned from the window and asked, "Mom, aren't we going to talk about the fire?" His eyes jerked back and forth from Beth to Izzy. "Don't you want to know what caused it?"

Beth scooted forward on the edge of the couch. "Izzy and I were wondering the same thing." She turned to Mom. "Are we getting another trailer?"

"Hey, maybe there was some kind of guarantee," Michael said. "You know, if the wiring was bad or something was wrong with the furnace. The trailer company has to give us a new one. Don't they?"

Izzy picked at a hangnail on her thumb. It stung, but she kept pulling on the loose skin until a drop of blood stained her jeans.

The pop machine hummed. Maverick's collar jingled when he scratched. Mom looked at the dog lying on his blankets like she was surprised to see him. Then she turned to Beth.

"There won't be a new trailer. Accept the fact that this is our home. For a while anyway." Mom stood and sighed. "And, there's no need talking about the fire, Michael. It happened, and we can't do anything about it. Your father's gone. We live here. You're all going to school tomorrow."

"But, Mom." Michael walked across the room to her.

It seemed strange that Mom had to tilt her chin up to look in his face.

"That's enough, Michael," she said. "We're not going to waste any more time on this." Izzy recognized Michael's stubborn expression, but he backed down.

He turned, and his eyes locked on Izzy's.

The fights.

Their dad dying.

Living in the back of the store.

The pain of it all showed on Michael's face. He was a little boy about to cry. Then he flipped a switch and the hurt was gone— replaced by a Dad-like scowl.

"I'm taking a shower," he said and took long steps toward the swinging door, "before somebody uses up all the hot water."

Mom cleared her throat and clapped her hands once. "Good idea. Get organized. No sense rushing in the morning."

Beth sniffed then followed him through the swinging door.

Izzy took deep breaths, pushing the words away that wanted to fly from her mouth.

Words that would ease the pressure.

Words that would make them all hate her.

A country song blared from the radio Grandpa gave them, and the sound of water bounced off the shower walls. Izzy concentrated on a cattle feed poster taped to the swinging door. On it, a brown and white Hereford grazed near a patch of sunflowers—the happy flowers.

"Izzy?" Mom quit clicking the computer keys to look at her. "You need to get your things ready for tomorrow."

Izzy nodded but stayed in the middle of the office.

The poster blurred.

Words formed.

Heart pounded.

"Mom?"

Her mother turned. The fear and pain in her eyes, so intense, it took Izzy's breath. She swallowed the confession that had been building.

Instead, she said.

"I wish I had my lucky denim skirt to wear tomorrow."

CHAPTER 12

I zzy drew cat pictures in the window fog while she waited for the bus. It was the same bus as always, but she felt unsettled and edgy. She glanced at the clock above Mom's desk and wrapped herself in Dad's coat—surprised his scent was still so strong in the fabric—curious about her own need to keep wearing it.

Brakes squealed, and the bus stopped in front of the alley next to the store.

"It's here, Mom. Bye." After pulling the office door shut and walking toward the bus, Izzy turned to look down the alley. The cat sat at the corner of the theater. Green eyes staring, pulling at her. All sound muted except the same haunting song she had heard behind the theater a few nights before.

What'll I do? Hm, hmmm.

Izzy moved in the cat's direction.

Hm, hm, hm hmmm. And I'm so blue. A shiver crawled up her back. She crawled deeper into the coat.

Honk! Honk!

"Are you riding or not?" hollered Mrs. Mackelhaney.

Warmth colored Izzy's cheeks.

"Be right there," she said.

One more glance, but the cat was gone.

Izzy climbed onto the bus. Tugging on the coat's hood. Trying to hide from the dozen pair of sleepy eyes waiting to stare.

Mrs. Mackelhaney pulled the door shut behind her and said in her gravelly voice, "Sorry to hear about your dad."

Izzy nodded and plopped into the front seat. For once, she was glad Ariel and Jody didn't ride in the morning. She wasn't ready to see them yet. To answer their questions.

Mrs. Mackelhaney watched from the mirror just above the windshield. The fourth-grade girls in the seat beside Izzy stared with their mouths open. She was a freak.

Was this how it was going to be—everyone either too nice or just staring? Izzy counted the pink foam curlers covering Mrs. Mackelhaney's head. Thirteen, just like always. The driver looked up again and smiled. There was red lipstick on her front tooth, just like always. The bus turned right onto Main Street and roared toward the school on the highway, just like always. Still, it felt like someone else's life.

Izzy closed her eyes and rested her head against the window. The bus tires thumped and sang over the ridges in the street.

Your fault.

Your fault.

Your fault.

****

Streaks of rosy light peaked over the edge of the horizon, quickly swallowed by heavy clouds. Exhaust fumes soaked the air and fogged the buses and cars squealing into line in front of the school.

Everything was dull and muted, including the zombie-like parade shuffling into the school.

Just inside the building, Izzy squinted at bright fluorescent lights. The elementary hall was still heavy with Valentine's pictures. Sixth-grade science fair projects filled tables in the opposite hall. Just like they did almost two weeks ago. Nothing had changed, and everything had.

She had wanted to train Maverick to get the paper from the sidewalk in front of the store for her project.

"You leave Maverick alone," Dad had said.

Izzy's backup was to do something with Mom's plants. She closed her eyes and pictured the plants, black and curling in flames.

The smell of disinfectant from the janitor's mop bucket mingled with pancake syrup from the cafeteria. Izzy repeatedly swallowed to keep down the oatmeal Mom made her eat. She zigzagged through the cafeteria tables toward the school office to turn in the note Mom gave her.

A chaos of voices and phones rushed at her when she opened the glass door.

"Mary, can you get that phone?"

"Oops. Sorry. That was the intercom."

"I need to talk to the principal about my son's grades."

"Here's the key. Mrs. Robbins left her lesson plans on her desk."

Suddenly all voices stopped. A wave of faces turned to her with the same unsettled expression. What do you say to the girl who lost her home and her father?

Mrs. Robey hurried around the counter. "I am so sorry about your dad, Izzy," she said softly. Izzy tried to focus on the smell of peppermint on the secretary's breath rather than the choking tightness in her throat.

CHAPTER 13

Four, five, six, seven...

Izzy pulled the hood of her father's jacket tighter and counted her steps across the green cafeteria tile.

Fourteen, fifteen, sixteen...onto the stained carpet of the halls.

Thirty-one, thirty-two...past a side exit door.

How many steps back to the store? To the alley? To anywhere but here?

A slamming door and a familiar muttering distracted her from the urge to bolt. Jody was searching through her overstuffed locker. Izzy stepped over a pile of books and papers just as Ariel rounded the corner.

"Izzy, you're back!" Ariel tripped over a book while grabbing her in a hug.

Jody put her hand on Izzy's shoulder and said, "I'm sorry about your dad."

"Thanks," Izzy said.

"Yeah," Ariel said. "We missed you."

Thousands of conversations flooded Izzy's mind— notes passed in class, late-night whisperings, secrets told only to one another. They'd shared everything. Izzy ached to release the horrible secret she carried with her like a bag of sharp rocks.

"You feel alright?" asked Ariel. "You look kinda sick."

Ariel's words had a muffled, underwater kind of sound. Izzy leaned against the lockers and just nodded.

Think, she told herself.

Ask about classes or Jody's new earrings. Anything.

Just.

Don't.

Tell.

Izzy attempted a smile. "I'm fine. So, have I missed anything?"

"Bunches!" said Jody. "You'll never believe..."

The speaker above their heads crackled, "Student Council meeting in two minutes. Don't be late."

"Crud, gotta go." Jody shoved everything back into her locker. She hollered over her shoulder, "I'm alternate for homeroom."

Izzy bit her lip. Maybe she could just tell Ariel. Maybe the sharp ache would be better if someone else knew.

"Ariel, I need to..."

"Oh, my gosh!" Ariel said, "I'm supposed to sell yearbooks in the cafeteria after morning assembly. We'll talk at lunch. Okay?"

Izzy watched Ariel disappear around the corner. Turning to go to her locker, she tried to ignore the dull pain behind her eyes, the tightness in her throat, and the theater song that had followed her to school.

****

Fourth hour, just before lunch, Izzy was halfway through some make-up chapter questions about Argentina's exports when she heard her teacher's soft voice.

"Izzy, could I speak with you?"

She glanced at Ariel. Her friend shrugged her shoulders and stood to sharpen her pencil. Ms. Gale pulled an extra chair beside her desk.

This can't be good, Izzy thought. She dropped onto the chair—grateful she didn't have to trust her trembling legs.

"I know it has to be tough coming back to school after the loss you've experienced."

No, not now! I don't want to talk about this, Izzy screamed inside her own head. Then she startled, fearing she'd said it out loud.

The pencil someone was tapping went silent, and the new boy in the corner stopped whispering to himself. Ms. Gale's words sounded underwater muffled like Ariel's did in the hall. Izzy gripped the sides of the chair as the classroom tilted.

Suddenly, Ms. Gale's face came back into focus.

"I want you to have this." She reached for a plastic sack. "Maybe it will help."

Izzy scanned the room to see if anyone was watching. Ariel and Jody looked up, then back to their test papers.

"Use it now, if you want." Ms. Gale smiled, tears in her eyes. "Or, you can save it for later." She patted Izzy's back then shuffled papers on her desk.

"Uh, thank you," Izzy said.

Hoping her rubbery legs would keep working while she walked back to her desk. She wondered what was in the bag but knew she had to be alone before she could look.

CHAPTER 14

66 That test was really hard, didn't you think?" Jody asked and then bit her thumbnail.

"Not if you studied, Jody," Ariel said. "Didn't you use those flash cards we made?"

Jody giggled and said, "Nope, I was on the phone." She did a little twirl in the hall. Ariel reached in front of Izzy and grabbed Jody's arm.

"You're kidding me. Did you really stay on the phone that long?"

"What are you talking about?" Izzy asked. They ignored her and squealed.

"Didn't your folks get mad, Jody?" Ariel linked her arm with Jody's, and they kept walking while Izzy stopped in the hall.

"Hey, what's going on?" she said, hating the quiver in her voice.

"Oh, that's right," Jody said. "You weren't here." She came back and grabbed Izzy's arm. "We'll show you at lunch." Ariel and Jody giggled again.

Ariel grabbed Izzy's other arm and said, "Let's hurry before all the pizza's gone."

"No," Izzy said. "I'll meet you at our table." She turned before one of her friends offered to pay. She didn't turn soon enough to miss their sad expressions. Just like the bus driver that morning, and Mrs.

72

Robey, and everyone who didn't know what to say to poor Izzy. She grabbed a tray of mystery meat and mushy peas in the free lunch line and weaved her way through rows of tables.

One, two, three...Izzy counted her steps to the perfect spot.

Five, six, seven...to the table across from the milk cooler.

Ten, eleven, twelve...to her friends.

To normal.

Her head shot up when she heard Jody's, *there's-a-cute-guy-around,* giggle. Two boys sat across from Ariel and Jody, but no place was left for her. She stood there like a jerk for a few seconds, then backed away.

"Oh, Izzy," Ariel said, her face bright red. "Uh, I guess things filled up before... I'll sit with you at another table."

"Nnno," Izzy stammered. "That's okay. I see a seat over there. Uh, I'll talk to you later." She turned and hurried to dump her food in the trash. So much for school making things feel normal again.

****

"It was so great, Mom. Really. I didn't want to go back yet, but," Izzy leaned down to kiss her mom's cheek, "I'm really glad I did."

It was an Academy Award performance.

Mom's smile made the lie worth it.

After supper, Izzy sat cross-legged on her bed, plowing through make-up schoolwork. Her fingers touched Ms. Gale's plastic bag when she searched the backpack for an eraser. She aimed the opening of the sack toward the dim light. Her breath caught in her throat when a bright yellow sunflower winked from the front of a new blue spiral. Clipped to the twisting metal on the edge of the notebook was a green gel pen with a sunflower glued on top. She couldn't get the pen cap off fast enough. She flipped to the first page and wrote:

Favorite Teachers

1. Ms. Gale

Izzy loved the grassy color of the ink flowing onto the paper. She turned to the next page and smiled at the sound of paper crinkling. She wrote **The Old Theater** and reached under her pillow to search for the notes she'd written on paper borrowed from Mom's printer.

"Lights out, everyone," Mom called from the kitchen.

Beth shut off the light. Izzy groaned. She slipped the paper between pages of the notebook and pushed the pen through the metal loops. After sliding everything under her pillow for safekeeping, she lay back and listened.

Maverick whined from the office. His tags clinked, and she knew he was turning in circles on his blanket, finding a sleeping spot. Michael coughed, Beth sighed, and soft words came from the kitchen. Mom was talking to someone on the cell phone—probably Grandma. Across the street, the train rumbled over the tracks, its lonely whistle fading away. The sound reminded her of the last night in the trailer.

She slipped her hand under her pillow till her fingertips touched the raised surface of the flower on the notebook. For just a little bit, the tightness in her chest relaxed.

She could breathe.

Sleep came.

Dreams followed.

CHAPTER 15

"We're sorry," said Ariel just before morning assembly the next day.

Jody squeezed into the spot on the other side of Izzy. "We don't blame you for being mad." She dropped her bag onto Izzy's foot. "We've decided..."

Ariel interrupted, "No more boys at lunch."

"They were kind of dorky anyway." Jody rolled her eyes. "They kept burping and snorting milk out their noses."

No one said anything for a little bit. Ariel jiggled her leg, then cleared her throat and said, "We're sorry about your dad."

"Yeah, it must be horrible," Jody added, "to have your dad die *and* live in the back of that yucky store."

"Jody!" Ariel hissed. "We just feel bad for you." She touched Izzy's arm. "It's hard to know what to say."

"It's okay," Izzy said. "I wouldn't know what to say to me either." She focused her eyes on a kid across the gym, tripping on someone's outstretched leg. She picked at her jagged thumbnail and wondered what Jody would say if she knew Dad was passed out drunk that night.

That the fire had been her fault.

That she'd heard a voice behind the unlocked door of the theater.

"Let's talk about something else," Izzy said.

"Okay," Ariel said. "We have a new litter of kittens in the barn."

"Oh! I love baby kittens," Jody said.

Izzy tried, but she couldn't keep up with the conversation. Jody's earlier words kept replaying. Then a buzzing swelled in her head. The sound changed to the hum of one long note then, "Hm, hm, hm, hmmm." Izzy swiveled her head to look for the source of the music.

She put her hand on Ariel's arm and asked, "Did you hear that?"

Izzy saw Ariel's forehead wrinkle and the look she gave Jody.

"That song. Can't you hear it?"

****

"I've got an idea," Ariel said at lunch. "Let's study Saturday for the science test.

Jody rolled her eyes. "Oh, that sounds like fun."

Izzy could see the hurt on Ariel's face, but she silently agreed with Jody.

"Well, I just thought it would be good to help Izzy," she said. "She missed a lot of class, but I bet they'll make her take that test. How about Saturday?"

"As much fun as studying sounds," Jody said with a sarcastic tone, "my family's going to Topeka."

"Studying sounds good to me," Izzy said. "You can come to the store. It'll be fun." Then she remembered Jody's words about living in the back of the store. She grabbed Ariel's arm. "Hey, if it isn't too cold, we can have a picnic in the park across the street."

Ariel's idea was to study, but the theater would be right across from the park. Just waiting. If Izzy could keep from chickening out, her real plan involved an old building and a flashlight.

CHAPTER 16

Sunlight glinted off the wings of a lone jet, miles beyond the earth. Its vapor trail painted a white slash above the Kansas landscape.

Above cornfields and gravel roads.

Above the city park, where two girls struggled to make the afternoon something they could brag to Jody about on Monday. Birds pecked at the crumbs from their PBJ lunch on the picnic table, and the studying had begun.

"Here goes." Izzy made a dramatic throat-clearing. "Name the six simple machines."

Ariel pushed back with her legs on the swing. "OK, there's a lever, wheel and axle, uh, screw, pulley, and inclined plane." She pumped through the air and threw her head back.

Izzy made a game-show buzzer sound. "Wrong!"

Dust rose around Ariel when she stopped swinging. "How can that be wrong? There are six."

Izzy pumped her swing higher. "You only said five."

"Did not!"

Ariel hated to be wrong.

"Whatever." Izzy quit pumping on the swing. It slowed to a stop, and she looked across the street at the weather vane spinning on the theater's roof. The hairs on her arms prickled when she thought she saw a shadow move across one of the top floor windows. She shook off the feeling and turned back to Ariel, "You ask me a question."

"OK. What is kinetic energy?"

Izzy smiled as she watched Ariel twisting the swing's chain then spinning when she let go.

"You are."

Ariel stopped twirling. "Hey, you're right."

Maverick's barks sounded from where he had been asleep in the shade of the feed store building.

"Hush, Maverick!" Izzy hollered. "I wondered what woke him up?"

"Oouuw! What was that?" Ariel jumped from the swing.

"Meow."

Izzy reached for the cat at Ariel's feet and held it close. "Well, no doubt you are bugging Maverick again. This is that cat I told you about. You know, the one Maverick chased the night I heard the thumping and the voice."

"You mean the night you heard Dirty Bertie talking?" Ariel touched the cat's head with cautious fingers.

"Yeah, I'm sure it's the same one." The long fur was soft on Izzy's cheek. "Aren't you pretty?" The cat stretched its head around and stared into Izzy's eyes. It jumped from her arms and streaked across the street.

"Come on," Izzy said. "I think it's going back to the theater." The girls waited for a car to pass then raced into the alley and to the back of the building.

The cat was waiting for them on the hood of the rusted car like it had done it a thousand times. "Here, kitty-kitty," said Izzy.

"Meow."

In one fluid motion, the cat jumped from the car and slipped through a hole at the bottom of the brick wall.

"You want to see if the door will open?" Part of her longed for Ariel to say no.

Ariel's voice sounded wobbly. "Are you sure you want to go in there, Izzy? It's so creepy, and you are the biggest chicken I know."

"Look who's talking," Izzy grinned, then got serious.

"I can't explain it. I just have to see inside." She grabbed her friend's sweaty hand. "It'll probably be locked anyway."

It wasn't.

The handle turned easily, but Izzy had to push hard on the door as it scritched on the gritty floor. Beyond the door, the building was pitch black. "Wait here. I'm getting a light." Izzy jumped over the weeds to get the big flashlight from the feed truck.

"No way. You're not leaving me here alone." Ariel was barely out of the weeds before Izzy came running back.

"This is cool—kind of like those books we read about teenage spies," Izzy said.

A hollowness widened in her chest when she remembered there wouldn't be any more of those books. She ignored the hurt and used her hip to force the door open more, releasing dust and musty air.

"Awck!" Ariel wrinkled her nose. "Do you think this place is haunted like everybody says?"

"All I know is someone was right where we're standing the night Maverick chased the grey cat," Izzy whispered. Her thighs began trembling, but she led on.

Their feet stirred more dust, and it danced in the flashlight beam. Izzy pointed the light into a narrow hall.

"Why is it so cold in here?" asked Ariel. "I'm freezing."

Izzy felt Ariel's fingers squeezing her sweatshirt in the back.

"Don't know. Maybe someone left the air conditioner on for the last hundred years." Izzy's nervous giggle echoed.

"Yeah, right," Ariel said. They shuffled behind the light beam.

Thump, thump, thump.

"What's that?" Ariel whispered near Izzy's ear.

"Ouuuu! Maybe it's Dirty Bertie's broom." Izzy was making a joke, but it didn't seem as funny as she thought it would.

Thump, thump, thump. The sound was moving closer.

Ariel stopped and pulled Izzy's arm.

"Hey, you're blinding me." Ariel reached for the light and pushed it down. It slipped from Izzy's fingers and rolled across the floor with flitting shadows. It clanked against the wall blinking off and on. Izzy stooped to pick it up and slapped it against the palm of her hand. The light blinked again but then showed its full power.

"Whishu. That was close." Izzy turned to smile at Ariel. The smile stopped when she saw Ariel's face go pale.

"It's okay, Ariel. The light's working fine. See?" Izzy directed the beam ahead of them, into the hall, and up the ceiling, where a dinosaur-shaped stain spread out from the inside wall.

"Look," Ariel's yelped. She grabbed Izzy's arm and directed the light to the left and down.

There in the dusty beam was a distorted face.

"AAAWWWHHH!" Both girls screamed. The flashlight clunked to the floor and rolled further into the hall.

"Go! Go!" Izzy shouted.

They slid on the dusty floor and slammed the door behind them. Ariel tore down the alley, but Izzy hesitated. She stopped in the middle of the alley, listening to the same tapping rhythm, now coming from the top of the building. Her fingertips traveled along the rough bricks—curiosity stronger than fear. She walked sideways with her eyes focused on the top of the theater.

The smart thing to do would be to never go into that creepy building again. Izzy listened to the thumping getting softer. A door slammed. Then another and another and another.

CHAPTER 17

At lunch on Monday, things seemed almost normal. Almost. The boys were burping for a new audience, and no one mentioned the fire. Not once.

It was perfect.

Until Ariel brought up Izzy's birthday.

"Mom's making a big deal about me going to some family thing in Nebraska around the same time. She told me to ask you what day your birthday party is." Ariel's eyes opened wide. "I know you can't have a big party, but..."

"No, it's okay. It won't be like before, but I'll ask Mom today."

She closed her eyes and pictured flames eating up her party list. "I'll let you know as soon as things are final." She stopped at the water fountain—hoping a drink would lessen the ache that wouldn't leave. The song from the theater flashed through her mind.

"The Street Fair Festival is right after Izzy's birthday," Jody said.

Ariel clapped her hands close to her chest, and Jody jumped up and down.

Izzy tried to show excitement like her friends. The Taggert Creek Street Fair was one of the most exciting times of the year in their little town. The park and most of Main Street would be full of rides, food, and all kinds of fun. Izzy thought it might be even better to be living just steps from it all. Or maybe not. Mom will probably say there's no money to waste on rides.

Izzy pulled her books and binder from her locker. The dark alley and the theater's back door flashed through her thoughts. Then the song. It darted from her mind to the back of her throat, where it vibrated into the air.

"What'll I do...hm, hm, hm, hmmm."

So beautiful.

So disturbing.

"See you after fifth hour," Izzy said, then turned and walked away.

She heard Jody whisper, "Did you hear her humming that song again? She's acting so weird."

"I know," Ariel said.

Their words stung, but Izzy kept weaving through the flow of students. She hurried past the door of her next class and ran to the only place she felt safe.

The muffled hush and scent of the library greeted Izzy like her best friend. She scanned the open area and spotted the librarian on the phone in her office. Izzy walked to the fiction section, running her fingers along the book spines. Maybe she could get a book and read just one chapter. Maybe this once. Her eyes zeroed in on new books on a cart, ready to be shelved. The covers were unscratched and beautiful. She had to read textbooks or her grades would drop, but so far, she'd kept the promise to not read the books she loved.

The books that made her dad so mad.

That made her light the candle.

The muscles in her arm twitched, and her fingers grazed the cart. A static shock snapped between the metal and her fingers.

"Ouch!" Izzy pulled her hand away and backed from the shelf. That was close.

She wondered what would happen if she'd stopped her no-book punishment.

When she slipped into her English classroom, Mrs. Myers was getting excited about possessive nouns.

Izzy pretended to listen.

CHAPTER 18

"Mom, do you know something special that's going to happen next month?"

On the bus trip home, Izzy had composed and rearranged the question Ariel and Jody had been bugging her to ask. Now, watching her mom's smile fade, she knew she should have swallowed the words.

Too late.

Mom slammed a drawer shut then said, "I know there will be more bills coming in, but that isn't special."

"No, I mean in our *family*. Do you know what special day in our family?" Izzy tried to sit on her mom's lap but changed her mind and lost her balance. She grabbed the side of the desk. A stack of papers went flying.

"Oh, Izzy. I just had those sorted." Mom kneeled to retrieve them. "I don't have time for guessing games, and neither do you. You need to finish your homework, then file these papers for me."

"I got it done on the bus." Izzy bit into her pinky nail.

"Okay," Mom said. "Take Maverick for a quick walk, then start this filing."

Izzy grabbed Maverick's leash and snapped it to his collar—glad to escape the question she'd left hanging.

"Let's go, boy."

Maverick dragged her out the door and then stopped to sniff the air.

Izzy turned when she heard Michael grunting with the weight of the fifty-pound sack he was lifting onto the feed truck. He seemed older since the fire, more serious. She remembered how he saved Beth and her.

"Hey, Michael," Izzy hollered.

He kept stacking. Izzy herded Maverick to the truck and tapped her brother on the shoulder. "Michael?"

"What?" He panted then wiped his forehead with his sleeve.

"You should take Maverick with you on the feed delivery. Dad always did. She kneeled to wrap her arm around the dog's broad back. "I think he misses it."

Michael hesitated, then dropped beside Maverick. "Hey, you smelly dog. You want a ride in the truck?" He rubbed the dog's ears, and they both smiled when a contented moan vibrated from deep inside Maverick's chest.

Michael stood, "Take him in the vacant lot, and by the time he's finished, I'll be ready to leave." The loading dolly's wheels squeaked as he pushed it into the feed storage building.

Izzy hurried the dog through his leg lifting, and they both trotted to the truck. Michael was fiddling with the radio when Maverick jumped onto the seat beside him. Michael smiled, Maverick sniffed, and Izzy felt like she'd finally done something right.

She stepped back when the truck rolled from the curb in a cloud of exhaust. A grey blur bolted from behind the wheels and into the alley.

"Hey, kitty."

The cat slowed then weaved its way through the dried weeds—her paws touching the ground with delicate steps. Izzy followed, then hesitated halfway through the alley. The angle of the sun spotlighted some words written on the bricks. It was just over her head under a high boarded-up window. She stretched to get a closer look and ran her fingers lightly across the carved words.

B-E-R-T-I-E A-N-D T-O-M 1943

Cooing and fluttering from the theater's roof distracted her.

Thump. Thump. Thump.

Izzy used her fingertip to trace the first name on the brick. "Is that you Dirty Bertie?" she whispered. At that moment, with the feed truck roaring into the distance, she knew she had two problems—her birthday and a nagging urge to explore the theater.

CHAPTER 19

"Stop before you go any further." Mom wiped her wet hands on a dishtowel. Izzy hadn't meant to say anything about her birthday until Mom was in a better mood, but she couldn't put off Ariel and Jody any longer.

"Surely you understand." Mom said. "There's not enough money to pay the bills, let alone some fancy birthday party." Her voice was thin and tight like a rubber band stretched to the point of breaking. She leaned down to open the small refrigerator. "I can't even keep enough milk for you kids to drink." She slammed the door causing the stack of bowls on top to rattle. "Clean up your mess when you're done." Mom walked the few feet to the cramped bathroom and pulled the folding door so hard, part of it fell from the track. Thunder rumbled in the distance.

Izzy sat at the table staring at the graham cracker in her hand. Her chest hurt, knowing her mom was upset. She knew there wasn't money for a big party. What she had planned wouldn't cost hardly anything. She grabbed her new sunflower notebook and ruffled the pages until she found the list.

Invite Ariel and Jody

Cake and maybe ice cream.

Tell them to eat supper before they come.

Izzy pushed her hand to the bottom of her bag in search of the green pen. She didn't notice Beth slip up behind.

"Hey, what's this?" Beth grabbed the notebook from the table and started reading it out loud. "Number one, invite Ariel and Jody…"

"Give it back, Beth," Izzy hissed. She wished her sister would go back to not talking. "Mom! Make her give it back." Izzy tried to grab the notebook, but Beth held it out of her reach.

"Number two, cake and maybe ice cream." Beth tossed the notebook on the table. "Mom said the kind of shampoo I want is too expensive. Do you think she's going to let you have a party?"

Mom walked from the bathroom just as another clap of thunder made them all jump. "What are you two fighting about now?" She grabbed the notebook from the table.

"It's mine, Mom," Izzy said. Then softer, "It's mine." Mom's eyes scanned the words. She ripped the sheet from the spiral binding. Izzy felt a rip in her heart.

"I told you there wasn't going to be a party. Just get it out of your head." She slammed the notebook on the table, then folded Izzy's plans and pushed the paper into her jeans pocket. "Beth, get busy sweeping the office, and Izzy, I'll be in your room to talk to you. Go!"

Izzy's eyes burned, but she wouldn't give Beth the satisfaction of seeing her cry. She grabbed the notebook and ran to her so-called room. When she dropped onto the top bunk, another boom of thunder rattled the roof. Izzy curled into a tight ball, listening to rain pelting above her head. Then she heard Mom's voice beside her.

"Sit up."

Mom's words—so soft, so sad. Izzy glanced into Mom's face and wiped her nose on the back of her hand.

"You've got to listen to me now," her mom said. "We don't have the money for a party. And frankly, I'm just not up to it since your dad, since the fire." Mom got a far-away look in her eyes. "I'm sorry. I know you want your birthday to be special, but I'll make you a cake. Wait, no oven." Mom bit her lip. "I'll get you one of those cakes from the store and fix something special for supper, but no sleepover. Do you understand?"

Izzy remembered the lop-sided cake she'd made Dad on his last birthday. He'd eaten it but never said thank you. Why couldn't she just remember the good stuff about him?

Mom lifted Izzy's chin. "Tell me you understand."

Izzy knew Mom was right. But weren't birthdays supposed to be special? It wasn't like she could repeat her twelfth birthday next year.

"Isabel?" Mom's voice was a little stronger.

Izzy nodded, not because she was willing to give up, but because Mom needed her to agree. She dropped her head and looked through her hair to watch Mom leave the room

Hm-hm-hm-hmmm, when you are far away... The melody floated into Izzy's thoughts and pushed aside everything else. *Hm-hmmm, hm-hmmm, hm-hm-hm, hmmm.* She closed her eyes and pictured her body floating, gliding through a fog in the alley. The coarseness of the Bertie and Tom brick grazed her fingertips as she reached to touch it. Rounding the corner by the rusted car, looking into Cleopatra's glowing eyes, Izzy felt her body drift beyond the open door. The dark theater swallowed her like a giant beast.

"Hey!"

Izzy's eyes flew open. Beth poked her arm.

"Wake up," she said. "Mom said supper's ready."

"I was asleep? How long?" Izzy rolled off the top bunk and rubbed her eyes.

Beth stood with her hands on her hips. "Long enough for me to do all your work." She pointed her index finger at Izzy's face. "You're doing the dishes *alone* tonight." Beth glanced at her hair in the mirror and left the room.

Prickles of sweat formed under Izzy's bangs, and a shiver ran through her like ice water. So much was churning in her brain, she winced with the pain of it.

Time to talk to Ariel.

CHAPTER 20

I zzy sat on Beth's bed, tapping her feet and wondering how she could call Ariel without Mom hearing. Beth and Michael had gone to the Friday night basketball game with Michael's friend, so they wouldn't be a problem. Izzy startled when she heard Mom's voice from the other side of the plywood wall.

"Izzy," Mom called, "don't wait too late to take Maverick for his walk."

"I know. I'll go now," Izzy said.

Maverick sat on his haunches by the front office door. "You ready to go out, boy?" Izzy hugged his head against her leg. She grabbed the leash from the hook and noticed Dad's cell phone on the edge of the counter. A quick glance to see if Mom was watching, and she slipped it into her coat pocket. Maverick whined and pranced in front of the door.

"Sorry. Let's go." Izzy opened the door and raced to keep up with him. While he was sniffing out the perfect spot in the vacant lot, Izzy punched in Ariel's number.

"Hello," said Ariel's mom.

"Hi, it's Izzy. Can I speak to Ariel, please?" Izzy paced back and forth as far as the leash would allow.

"You bet. The girls are upstairs. Just a minute."

Girls? What girls? Izzy heard muffled words and then a click.

"I got it, Mom," Ariel sounded out of breath. There was music in the background. "Hello."

"Uh, hi," Izzy's words came out in a whisper.

"Hello? I can't hear."

It sounded like Ariel put her hand over the phone, but Izzy could understand.

"Hey, Jody. Turn the music down. I can't hear." The music stopped. "Sorry, who is this?"

She had no words. Her friends were having fun without her. She punched the off button and dragged a reluctant Maverick back to the office. Dad's favorite ring tone, "Take This Job and Shove It," sounded again from the phone just as Izzy set it on the counter. She wondered if Mom was ever going to change it. Izzy ignored the second and third ring while she took her time unhooking Maverick from the leash.

Mom called from the back, "Answer that, would you?" The song phrase played a few more times until it stopped. Mom's voice came closer. "Izzy, didn't you hear me?"

"Sorry, couldn't get to it in time." She bolted to her room and was climbing to the top bunk when the song on the phone sounded again.

"Hello. Yes, she's right here. Just a minute." Mom followed Izzy and handed her the phone. "It's Ariel."

"Oh, good. Thanks." Izzy's smile felt pasted on her lips. She waited until she heard the squeak of the swinging door. "Hello."

"Why did you hang up?" Ariel said.

"What are you talking about?" Izzy jumped from her bed and paced back and forth.

"Oh, come on, Izzy. Haven't you ever heard of caller ID?" Ariel's voice had an edge. "Why did you call and then hang up?"

"You sounded really busy with Jody and all." Izzy hated the ugly sneer she saw in the wavy mirror as she walked by.

"Oh, that. Let me explain..."

"Ariel, can I try on these jeans?" Izzy recognized Jody's voice.

"Like I said," Izzy spit out the words, "you're busy. So maybe I'll see you Monday." She hit the off button and stopped herself before she threw the phone against the wall. Instead, she threw her pillow.

"Traitor!"

In the kitchen, she set the phone on the table a little harder than she intended. She longed for a door to slam but settled for flipping the curtain over her bedroom doorway.

It wasn't the same.

She shut off the light and lay staring at the dark ceiling.

Playing the phone conversation over and over.

Aching for a book.

****

Izzy avoided Ariel at school, but fourth hour, there was no ditching her *former* best friend. A triangle folded note came flying onto her desk when Ms. Gale wrestled with the wall map. Izzy picked up the note, prepared to throw it back, but Ms. Gale turned to face the class. Curiosity pushed her to slowly unfold the paper. She slipped it behind her textbook and pretended fascination with the rain forests of Peru while she read the words.

You didn't let me explain. Jody's mom called Friday night and said she had to take Jody's grandma to the emergency room. She asked if Jody could spend the night. I know you think we planned something without you, but we didn't—I promise. Jody's at the hospital now.

See you at lunch???

BFF Ariel

Izzy felt a burning creep up her neck to her cheeks. She turned and connected with Ariel's eyes. "I'm sorry," she mouthed.

Ariel whispered, "Me too."

The bell rang, and the girls met in the hall. "I'm sorry I was such a jerk," Izzy said and hugged Ariel.

"Oh, I wouldn't say a jerk—how about dork?" Ariel pulled Izzy along. "Hurry up, or we won't have time to eat. I'm starved."

Izzy felt bad about Jody's grandma, but it was a perfect time to talk without her. She mumbled around the last bite of cheeseburger. "I want to talk about the theater."

Ariel's eyes widened. "I've been dying to say something, but it's hard since you don't want Jody to know." She looked straight at Izzy. "Tell me again. Why can't we tell her?"

"Because we don't want our parents to find out. Let's not go over that again." Izzy glanced at the clock on the wall. "We need to go into the theater again."

"You mean past that hideous *whatever* we saw?" Ariel shivered. "If that was Dirty Bertie, she's one ugly old lady."

"Yeah, but I've been thinking. It didn't seem like a real face to me." The girls stood and started toward the trashcans.

"So," Izzy asked as they headed toward their lockers, "when can you come over?"

"I'll ask my mom and call you tonight," Ariel said.

"Bring a flashlight," Izzy called after her. Ariel held up her right thumb and kept walking.

Izzy pulled open her locker, then stood staring into it. She didn't think the hideous face would be as scary since they would be expecting it. But. Whatever was beyond that made her heart pound.

CHAPTER 21

The theater's weathervane squeaked in a cool breeze that hinted at spring. With each turn, the metal cat on top seemed to steal glimpses of the two girls sitting on the curb in front of Dunn's Feed Store. They thought they were alone—unaware of shadowed eyes watching from the theater's top floor windows.

"Mom says, no birthday sleepover," Izzy said. She picked up pieces of gravel and tossed them, one at a time, into the street. "My grades aren't that great. Maybe if I promise I'll work harder, she'll let me invite just you."

"Awesome," Ariel said. "I've never spent the night in a store."

"Trust me, it's not that awesome—unless you have a thing for cricket chirps all night and mice running across the floor."

By the look on Ariel's face, Izzy realized she'd revealed too much. She jumped to her feet and said, "Hey! Did you bring the flashlight?"

"Got it right here." Ariel pulled a small light from her pocket.

"Good," Izzy said, then craned her neck to see if Mom was watching. "Promise. We keep going no matter what," she said, then started into the shade of the alley.

"Agreed," Ariel said. "But, we could wait for another day. You know, if you want."

Izzy pivoted. "Are you kidding?"

"No, I just thought. If you're too scared."

Izzy grabbed Ariel's arm and was glad her friend didn't know how much her heart was pounding. "Come on. Let's go."

They slid to a stop at the end of the alley. Izzy tried to steady her trembling hand when she grabbed the backdoor handle. "Ready?" She didn't wait for an answer. She turned the handle and shoved. The door scraped across the floor. "You go in front since you have the light," Izzy said. "That way, I can push you through if you get scared." Izzy gave Ariel a little shove and smiled.

"Yah, yah," said Ariel. "I remember you running just as fast as I did last time."

"Whatever. Let's get going before someone sees us."

The light beam sliced through the dusty air. Sunlight and the girls were swallowed by darkness. The temperature plummeted.

"Don't drop the flashlight," Izzy instructed. Her words rattled through chattering teeth.

"There's the stain on the wall," Ariel whispered. "That face thing should be ahead." She scanned the light to the left, and both girls gasped when the face came into view.

"Keep the light steady, Ariel. I want to see what it is." The girls shuffled toward the life-sized figure sitting on a trunk in the corner.

"It's a pirate," Ariel said.

Izzy grabbed the flashlight from Ariel and moved closer. "I think it's some kind of mannequin," she said.

"But it looks so real," Ariel said. "That bald head kinda makes him look like your math teacher."

"Hey, you're right." Izzy tried to squelch her giggle. "Can you imagine Mr. Harris with that long greasy hair on the sides and one earring?" She reached out to touch the bluish veins on the pirate's hand, then moved the flashlight beam past the ragged military jacket and short pants. "Oh gross! He has toe fungus," she whispered.

"That is so disgusting." Ariel moved closer.

"Ahoy, matie," shouted the figure.

Izzy fell backward and scooted against the wall. Ariel screamed and ran.

"Argh. Ha, ha, ha!"

When the pirate's head turned toward Izzy with glowing eyes, she scrambled to her feet and ran.

"Wait for me!"

The pirate's coarse laugh echoed through the hall as Izzy slid around the corner and squinted into bright daylight. She caught Ariel at the end of the alley and pulled her into the feed storage building. They ran to the far corner and climbed to lie panting on a stack of feed.

"Well," Izzy said, "so much for not stopping." Their giggles echoed. "Ahoy, matie. Argh."

"Snort, snort." Ariel rolled to her stomach. "Stop, Izzy, stop. I can't breathe."

"Oh, my gosh," Izzy said, "How are we going to get past that ugly thing?"

Ariel turned with her mouth gaping. "What do you mean get past it? I'm not going in there again."

"Oh, yeah," Izzy said. "Me neither. That would be crazy."

CHAPTER 22

"Hmmm," Mom mumbled as she ran her finger down the grades on Izzy's report card. "Good, good."

"Mom?"

"Just a minute," she said. "I'm still looking."

"Mom?" Izzy clicked her thumbnail on her teeth while she waited for Mom to finish.

"Okay, Kiddo. Much better grades. You can invite *one* friend for your birthday."

"Really?!" Izzy squealed and wrapped her arms around her mom's neck. "Thank you, thank you." She scooped up her backpack from the floor then did a bouncing walk toward the swinging door. "Can I call Ariel? That's who I want to invite. Oh, she's not home right now. I'll tell her tomorrow." Izzy ran back and hugged Mom again.

"I'm glad you're happy," Mom said. "Get your homework done, so we don't have to go through this again."

Izzy ran to her room—grateful Beth was at a math club meeting. She threw her bag on Beth's bed and pulled out her notebook. The sunflower on the front made her smile. She kissed it and crawled to the top bunk. The pages crinkled as she shuffled them to find the birthday party list she'd rewritten.

Invite Ariel and Jody and maybe a couple other girls

Cake and maybe ice cream.

Borrow a blow-up mattress so we can sleep in the office and have some privacy.

The plan was to talk all night about anything except fires and her sad life.

Izzy drew a calendar in her spiral and marked off the days until May 15th. Fourteen days seemed like forever. She felt a nudge in the back of her thoughts.

Your fault.

Your fault.

Your fault.

She shook her head like a snow globe to erase the ugly words—rubbed her fingers across the happy sunflower—tried only to think about her special day.

But, it turned out, her happy day was everything but special. She could have filled pages in the spiral with everything that went wrong. From the beginning, it was a disaster.

CHAPTER 23

Disaster #1 - Mom startled Izzy awake on her birthday morning. "The bus is honking! Hurry up!"

Every time she'd fallen asleep in the night, Izzy had seen the alley stretching out—a silhouette of her dad at the far end.

Izzy threw on some clothes, stuffed a piece of toast in her mouth, and looped her bag across her shoulders.

After the third set of honks, she stomped up the bus steps and mumbled through a mouth full of bread, "Sorry, Mrs. Mackelhaney."

"You better set that alarm a little earlier, Isabel Dunn." Everyone on the bus laughed. Izzy slipped into an empty seat and scrunched her body down with her knees against the back of the seat in front.

Barely making it before morning assembly began, Izzy plopped down between Ariel and Jody.

"Happy Birthday!" they both shouted. They sang the birthday song, and Izzy blew out her breath, not realizing she'd been nervous they might forget.

After the song, Jody slapped her palm against her forehead and said, "Oh, Izzy, I left your present on my bookshelf." Jody bit down on her thumbnail. "I'll bring it Monday."

"That's okay. Sorry I couldn't invite you both for tonight. Mom said just one."

"No biggie," Jody said. "Couldn't go anyway. My sister's getting some big award at college, and Mom's picking me up before lunch."

"Oh, that sounds like fun," Izzy said. She turned to Ariel. "Well, at least you'll be there. We're going to sleep in the front office so we can stay up as late as we want. And can you say, chocolate cake?"

Ariel smiled, but her eyebrows scrunched together. "Izzy, I need to tell you something."

"Good morning," said the principal.

"Good morning," everyone answered.

"I'll tell you at lunch," Ariel whispered.

Izzy leaned in to say something, but she caught sight of the social studies book open in her friend's lap.

Disaster #2 - "Oh, my gosh," Izzy whispered. "I didn't study for the test!"

The day only got worse.

Gross broccoli casserole stunk up the school all morning, making it difficult to get a full breath without nose wrinkling. Then worst of all, while Izzy ate her peaches and covered the broccoli with her napkin, Ariel delivered the news she'd been hinting at since morning assembly.

Disaster #3 - "Izzy, I need to tell you something." Ariel leaned in and whispered, "I can't spend the night."

"What?" Izzy's nervous giggle squeaked from her throat. "I thought you said..."

"I can't go home with you after school or stay the night." Ariel finally looked into Izzy's eyes. "I'm sorry."

"That isn't funny, Ariel," Izzy said. "You're kidding—right?"

Ariel shook her head.

Cafeteria sounds roared. Peaches stuck in Izzy's throat.

"Ariel, we've been planning this," she whispered. "It's my birthday."

"I know, but I told you Mom was planning a family thing in Nebraska. She says I have to go." Ariel chewed on her pinky's nail. "I can stay overnight some other time."

Izzy felt Ariel's cold fingers on her arm. "Don't be mad. It's not like you're having a party or anything," she said, then slipped from her seat.

Izzy kept her head down, picking at a hangnail.

"I've gotta go. Mom's checking me out early." She hesitated, then hollered over her shoulder as she weaved through the tables. "Have a good birthday."

Izzy sat staring at Ariel's back. A good birthday? "Is she kidding?" She slammed her knee on the table and hobbled to the closest bathroom—Ariel's words stinging.

It's not like you're having a party.

Not having a party.

Your fault.

Your fault.

Your fault.

CHAPTER 24

S pring raced across the fields with tiny shoots of green and the scent of damp earth and growing things. Baby calves kicked up their heels in pastures along the bus route. Izzy wished she could run with them.

Voices ricocheting off the bus walls made the seat beside her even more empty. She concentrated on a fly instead of the reason Ariel wasn't beside her. The fly pinged off the surface of the glass, searching for an escape. Izzy could have lowered the window to give it freedom but selfishly wanted it to stay. A wad of paper whizzed past her head and startled her buzzing friend.

She left without even saying goodbye.

Mrs. Mackelhaney skirted the bus around a slow farm tractor, then looked in the mirror and caught Izzy's eye.

"Bad day, Isabel Dunn?" she asked.

Izzy just nodded, not trusting her voice even to correct the name.

"Well, cheer up! Here's your stop, and you've got a whole weekend to celebrate your birthday. She handed Izzy a purple sucker and pushed her red lips into a huge smile.

"Thanks, Mrs. Mackelhaney." She wasn't sure how, but the bus driver always knew their birthdays. The bus door whished open, and a little piece of Izzy's misery melted away. She hurried into the feed store office, knowing her mom's words would melt even more.

Mom slammed the filing cabinet shut. "Oh, Izzy. Is school out already?" She ran her hand through her hair. "I've been swamped all day. Do you have homework?"

Izzy didn't answer.

"What's wrong?" Mom came around the counter. "Are you sick?"

Izzy dropped to the couch and tried to swallow the knot in her throat. She searched her mom's face to see if she was teasing like she'd hoped Ariel had been.

Disaster #4 - "Don't you remember? Mrs. Mackelhaney did." Her voice shook. "It's been a horrible day. They served broccoli casserole, Mom. Broccoli!" She stood and paced back and forth like a nervous cat.

"Stop now. You're not making sense." Mom turned to stack some papers on the desk. "Tell me what's wrong?"

"What's wrong? What's wrong is Ariel isn't spending the night." Izzy threw her arms in the air. "Of course, it's not like I'm having a party."

Mom's expression switched, and she raised her hand to cover her open mouth.

"Jody had a party with pizza, and skating, and a sleepover." She threw her bag against the side of a chair, causing it to tip. She knew she was being selfish, but she couldn't stop. "Ariel's parents built a *whole room* just for her." She let the hurt push her words. "What do I have? A plywood box I share with a sister who is perfect." She stopped. There was gunk in her throat, and she couldn't breathe.

Mom's fist came down hard on the counter.

"That's enough!" Her eyes were blazing, and Izzy knew she'd gone too far.

"One of these days, you're going to learn you can't have everything you want." Mom's face was pinched, and her lips trembled. "I didn't want your dad to die. I don't want to raise you kids alone in dark, cramped rooms with no privacy."

Mom's words cut her.

"But, you didn't tell me, happy birthday," she whispered, then ran from the store—unaware Maverick bolted through the open door behind her. She ran straight to Bertie and Tom's carved brick and slid down into bits of gravel and glass. Maverick nuzzled his cold nose under her arm.

"Oh, Maverick." She buried her face in his fur. He wriggled away with a whine and sprinted down the alley.

Disaster #5 - "Stop, Maverick!" She skidded around the corner in time to watch a dog-cat race disappear through the open back door of the old theater. Maverick's bark echoed from deep inside. "Maverick, get out of there!" She leaned into the doorway. A rush of coolness made the hair on her arms tingle. Sunshine showed the dusty floor, but beyond that, light vanished.

"Maverick," she said more softly, then slid down the wall just inside the door.

She doubled over with the pain of it all.

Rocked back and forth in the corner.

Moaned from so deep, it stole her breath and pushed her over the edge.

CHAPTER 25

Izzy was empty—spent and weak like she'd had the flu. She jerked when a sandpaper tongue scrubbed the back of her hand.

"Meow."

Thump, thump, thump.

The floor vibrated with the sound.

"Come, Cleopatra," said a shaky voice. "Let the girl be."

"Meow." Cleopatra stared into Izzy's eyes, blinked once, then flitted away.

Izzy pulled herself from the floor and shuffled to the darkness for a closer look. "Dirty Bertie?" she whispered. A chill traveled across her skin like someone had opened a freezer door.

At the edge of her vision, she saw a wooden box with black writing on the sides, and a faded blue cloth draped on top. A thick cookie sat on a chipped plate, and a metal cup beside it, filled with what she guessed was water.

Running her tongue over cracked lips, she reached for the cup. Cool and sweet—not water but apple juice. She mopped her mouth with the back of her hand and picked up the cookie. Looked homemade. Smelled like Christmas.

She took a small bite, then a bigger one, and another sip from the cup. It wasn't the best cookie she'd ever tasted but okay.

And what did she expect from a ghost?

"A ghost?!"

The metal cup clunked to the floor, splashing dust puddles against her legs. She stumbled from the theater, coughing to loosen the cookie that had lodged in her throat. She stopped in the alley and slapped her palms against the brick wall.

"Stupid! Stupid! Stupid!"

No doubt, she'd seen the ghost of Dirty Bertie.

No doubt the ghost had poisoned her with a Christmas cookie.

****

"Isabel Mae Dunn! Where have you been?" Mom's face was a scramble of anger and panic. "When Maverick came back alone, I sent Michael and Beth out looking for you.

Izzy wiped the sweat from her upper lip with the neck of her shirt. She didn't tell her mom not to call her Isabel.

"I went for a walk."

"A walk?" Mom collapsed into her desk chair. "You went for a walk."

Izzy lifted her shoulders in a deep sigh. She hated that she'd given Mom something else to make her forehead wrinkle.

"You look like you've taken a dust bath. Go wash your face." Mom pushed her hand through her hair. "Then come back here. We need to chat."

Izzy bit her lip and shouldered through the swinging door. Something twisted in her stomach. Mom would hurt even more when her youngest daughter died from a poisoned cookie.

She flipped on the light and shut the bathroom door. The mirror over the sink was old and wavy but was clear enough to show the dusty tracks on her cheeks. She filled the sink with water and splashed away the evidence before Michael and Beth saw.

Mom was locking up the cash register when Izzy slipped back into the office. "Feel better?" Mom asked.

Izzy nodded. Should she tell Mom or just wait for death?

"Good." Mom rolled her desk chair over to the old couch. "Sit and listen."

More stomach flutters.

Maybe she should tell.

Maybe there was some kind of medicine.

Maybe not.

Mom smiled, but Izzy could see her eyes were shiny. "Happy birthday, sweetheart." She fell into her arms, all forgiven.

"I know this birthday isn't what you wanted, but..." Mom stood and cleared her throat. "I wish things were different. We weren't in great shape before, and it's only worse since we lost your Dad."

Izzy ducked her head and picked at a hole in her jeans.

Mom grabbed her purse. "Now, I'm going to find Beth and Michael to tell them you haven't been kidnapped." She used her index finger to tap the end of Izzy's nose. "Then I'm going to the store to get your cake. I'll fix a nice supper, and we'll have candles on your cake and celebrate. That'll be fun, won't it?"

Izzy nodded. She wondered if she'd be alive when it came time for cake.

****

Izzy was still alive for the Frito chili pie, the birthday candles, and a huge piece of chocolate cake. She was shocked when presents appeared on the table. There was a new denim skirt from Mom. Beth and Michael gave her a shirt. It was orange, Beth's favorite color.

"Thanks. It's pretty," Izzy said. She felt guilty wishing it was blue. Maybe she'd save it for the last day of school—if she lived that long. At least, she wouldn't have to worry about taking end-of-the-year tests if the poison did its job soon.

CHAPTER 26

Agust front pushed through the town in the last few minutes before midnight. Lightening glowed in the distance, and the wind rattled the roof of the feed store like an invisible hand was shaking it.

Izzy wanted to sleep and forget the first day of her twelfth year, but it wasn't just the wind and Michael's snoring over the top of the thin walls that kept her awake. Her no-good-horrible day kept rushing back. She pushed her body onto her elbows to look at the clock on the dark wall.

"11:50—ugh," she whispered, then fell back on her pillow that still felt foreign.

Beth was grinding her teeth, and a cricket was chirping. She'd read somewhere that you could tell the temperature by the number of chirps a cricket makes.

"One…two…three," Izzy whispered. She stopped counting because she couldn't remember how long to count or what else you did. Another peek at the clock, 11:52.

Pushing back the sheet, she slipped from the top bunk. Her feet made soft slaps on the cold concrete floor. She stopped when Beth rolled over in her bed and mumbled something about a math problem. Only Beth would be dreaming about geometry.

The kitchen was dark except for a sliver of light under the swinging door. "Yee-ounch," Izzy hissed when a chair caught her little toe. She waited for the throbbing to stop, then opened the small refrigerator and used her fingers to dig out a chunk of cake. The frosting was cool and sweet and melted on her tongue. She swallowed and wondered why the poison hadn't made her sick yet. Maybe Dirty Bertie was just being nice. But could ghosts make cookies?

"That's crazy!" Izzy whispered. Ghosts don't make cookies. But, if she isn't a ghost, who is she?

A lightning strike made her jump. She slammed the fridge door shut and sprinted toward her room. Rain pelted against the roof, and the wind whistled like a voice.

"Isssaaa. Isssaaa. Isssabelllll..."

Izzy pivoted in all directions. "Who is that?" she hissed. But there was only the dark, and the wind, and her heart beating against her ribs. She scrambled to her bed, pulled the sheet over her head, and promised herself she wasn't ever going near that theater again.

She was wrong.

CHAPTER 27

Izzy survived the questionable cookies and the end-of-the-year tests at school. But sleeping late on the first morning of summer vacation didn't happen. Mom's conversation with a hearing-challenged farmer in the front office stole her *no bus honking* peace.

"Ugh!" she growled and slid from her bed. The air was spongy with humidity from someone's shower, but as always, the concrete floor felt almost icy. She pulled on clothes and grabbed her bag.

"Going to the feed building," she mumbled as she walked through the office.

"Okay, but just for a while." Mom said. "I have a job for you and Beth after she gets home from her sleepover."

No fair. All Izzy's friends had deserted.

Again.

Ariel was spending a couple weeks with her cousin in Nebraska, and Jody left yesterday for a month-long music camp.

Izzy kicked a piece of gravel. It bounced off the alley wall and woke Maverick from his nap under a rogue sunflower bush.

"Hey, Maverick," Izzy said, "you wanna come in the storage building with me?"

The dog raised his head like he was considering, then moaned and settled back into his shady spot.

"Fine," Izzy said. "Don't be whining to come in just as soon as I get busy in there." She reached down to pet his head.

Shuffling to the back corner of the building, she climbed to the highest stack of feed to catch a breeze from the open windows.

Stared at nothing.

Watched a wasp buzzing near the ceiling.

Tried to ignore the guilt pushing at her like a weight.

It wasn't just the fire anymore. She didn't miss Dad that much, and the shame of it made her cheeks burn. She did miss the way he *used* to be.

Turning on her stomach, she caught sight of the bricks across the ally. She'd tried to forget about the theater—to push it and everything else about the last few months out of her mind. But when she was alone, or at night after everyone was asleep, it consumed her. It was as if discovering the truth about the old woman would fix everything else.

She wrote on the top of a clean page in her sunflower spiral:

How to Find the Truth About Dirty Bertie.

Hide and watch for her. (might take too long)

Set up a camera and a wire to take her picture. (no camera—no wire)

Explore the rest of the theater and find her. (Too scary.)

?

Her mind went blank, and her legs were cramping. She slapped the notebook shut and made a leap off the stack of feed sacks. Her numb legs buckled, and she fell against one of the stacks.

"Hey, Izz." Michael hollered from the door. "You can't play in here. If you break open those feed sacks, we can't sell 'em." He pushed the loading cart through the door. It squeaked as it rolled.

"I wasn't playing," Izzy said. "And I'm not a baby. I was just thinking."

"Well, just don't tear things up in here while you're *thinking*."

She leaned back and watched Michael lift the heavy sacks and load them onto the cart. Before the fire, she and Michael used to joke around and play little tricks on Beth. Not anymore. Michael looked like Dad with his constant frown.

Izzy intended to ask about going swimming at Flory's pond, but that is not what came out of her mouth.

"Michael, if you were trying to catch a ghost, how would you do it?" she asked.

"What?" He pulled his t-shirt up to wipe the sweat from his face.

"Everybody says Dirty Bertie haunts the theater next door," Izzy said.

Dumb, dumb, dumb. Don't say anymore.

"I want to see if it's true. Can you help me?"

Michael rushed to push his face inches from hers. "Now you listen, Isabel Dunn." His eyes were wild, and spit flew with his words. "Stay out of that old building. You hear me?"

"Why?" Izzy backed away from him.

"You just do what I say. There's nothing there except that crazy old lady." He turned back to hoist one more sack onto his load.

"But, Michael…"

He pushed the dolly to the street, where she heard him grunting the sacks onto the truck.

"That was weird," Izzy said. She'd never thought about anyone else going in the theater. She watched her brother yank open the door of the truck. Just before he climbed into the seat, he glanced toward the windows under the theater's tower. His face went pale. He slammed the door. The truck tires threw gravel against the curb.

Someone had scared him. Bad.

Someone named, Dirty Bertie.

Someone Izzy was even more determined to see again.

CHAPTER 28

A car door slammed, and Izzy ran from the feed building. She squinted in the sun's glare to see Beth wave to her friend.

"Looks like you had fun," Izzy said.

Beth sighed.

"I did." Then she turned and narrowed her eyes at Izzy. "If you messed with my stuff while I was gone…"

"What stuff?" A giggle bubbled up in Izzy. "You don't have any more than I do."

Mom stepped from the store. "Think you girls can figure out how to put a cardboard display together? I need to make some phone calls." She pulled the cell phone from her pocket and went to the back rooms.

Beth dropped her things on the couch and immediately grabbed the instructions. "It says here to separate the cardboard pieces in ABC order. Stack them on the counter," she ordered. Izzy was glad Beth was talking again, even if she was being bossy. The only sound for a few minutes was cardboard squeaking and paper rattling.

"Piece 'A' goes on the bottom. Put it over by the wall where Mom wants the display," Beth said.

Dirty Bertie's song began looping through Izzy's thoughts. She came close to humming along with the notes but stopped herself and asked Beth the first thing that came into her mind.

"Beth," Izzy said. She pulled a piece of cardboard from the stack and laid it on the floor. "Do you believe in ghosts?" she asked, then almost swallowed her gum. If either Michael or Beth told Mom, Izzy would be grounded from ever going outside alone for the rest of her life, let alone near the theater.

Beth dropped the directions in her lap. "Izzy, Dad is not a ghost."

"No, that's not what I mean," Izzy said. "Do you think a ghost could open a door and do stuff like bake cookies?"

STOP TALKING! Izzy shouted inside her head.

Beth stared then shook her head. "I don't want to talk about ghost stuff. It creeps me out having to sleep in this dark old building without bringing up ghosts."

Mom shouted from the back rooms, "One of you girls, come help me quick."

"I'll go," Izzy said. It might be the only way she could keep from blurting out her secrets.

"What do you want, Mom?" Izzy asked.

Mom was on a stepladder, putting some things on a high shelf. "Hand me that bag of flour from the cabinet under the microwave. There's no need to take up space down there with no oven to bake anything." Izzy kneeled and found the sack of flour. She reached it up and felt her finger poke through the side of the sack. Mom tried to grab it, and Izzy tried to pull it back. The hole expanded. Flour rained all over Izzy's head and the floor below.

Mom sighed, then carefully climbed down. She stared at Izzy over her glasses.

Izzy released a nervous giggle and said, "Well, at least we don't have to worry about what to do with so much flour."

Mom didn't laugh.

"I'm sorry. I'll clean it up." She walked to the corner to get the broom and dustpan.

Mom's hands went to her head. "Stop, Izzy. You're tracking it everywhere."

All at once, Izzy knew exactly how to discover if Dirty Bertie was a ghost or a living, breathing human lady. Her brain raced through a perfect plan.

"Don't worry, Mom. I'll clean it up, and you'll never know it was there."

Mom mumbled to herself while she went back to the office.

Izzy swept the flour into the dustpan, then emptied the dirty flour into a plastic grocery sack. She scooped up the last piece of her birthday cake she'd been saving from the fridge and dropped it into a clean cottage cheese container. Watching through the crack beside the swinging door, she waited until Mom and Beth were distracted.

Izzy left a note by her mom's computer and slipped out the door. She ignored Maverick's whine and ran before Beth could stop her.

The air smelled of mowed grass and geraniums as Izzy rounded the corner of the feed storage building and into the alley. Cleopatra sat on the hood of the rusted car at the far end. Her eyes pulled at Izzy the whole time she walked down the canyon of brick walls.

"Here, kitty-kitty. Here, Cleopatra," Izzy said. Just before her fingertips touched the cat's head, Cleopatra blinked and darted from the car. Her body and graceful tail shimmied into the hole in the wall. Izzy shrugged and stepped through the weeds to the door. It stood ajar like it did when Izzy went inside on her birthday. Quick, before she changed her mind, she pushed the door open and walked into the little hall.

The wooden box was there, but the cloth, plate, and metal cup were gone. She didn't allow herself time to wonder where they'd gone but dropped the sack of flour to the floor and pulled out the cottage cheese container. Saliva filled her mouth when she pried off the lid and smelled the rich chocolate.

"It'll be worth the cake if I can find the truth about you, Dirty Bertie." The lid made a popping noise when Izzy slammed it back on the plastic container. She stepped forward and set her gift on the wooden box.

"Needs something else," she said to herself.

Back into the bright sunshine, she scanned the ground. A patch of tiny yellow flowers danced in the hot wind. The tough stems tore at her fingers, but she finally gathered a bouquet that made her smile. She found a rusty tomato can and filled it with water from the spigot behind the feed store. After stuffing the flowers into the can, she set the bouquet beside the cottage cheese container and stepped back to admire her work.

"That's better," she said. "Time to solve the mystery."

She sifted flour from the plastic sack around the box and all the way to the door. Surely a ghost *wouldn't* leave footprints.

Izzy stepped back into the sunshine and pulled the door the way she'd found it. The sound of cicadas clicking in the trees was so loud it made her ears ring. Sweat rolled down her back and made her hair stick to her neck. She folded up the sack and stuck it into the open window of the rusted car that stood like a guard.

"Hope this works," she mumbled.

"I think."

CHAPTER 29

"Ahhh," Izzy whispered when cool air and book smells met her inside the library. She stood with her eyes closed—tempted to go straight to the section she loved and open the first book her fingers touched.

"Excuse me."

Izzy stepped to the side and let Myrtle Bartlett in the door. Her arms were piled high with books. The smell of flowers and peppermint followed her into the library.

"Do you need some help, Mrs. Bartlett?" Izzy caught the top two books as they fell.

"Sure do, sweetie." She dropped the rest of the books onto the counter and peered over her glasses. "Oh, I almost didn't recognize you. You're one of the Dunn girls, aren't you?"

Izzy nodded and remembered Mrs. Bartlett saying she was only ten on the day of the funeral. "I'm Izzy."

"Isabel, isn't it? Sorry about your daddy," Mrs. Bartlett said. "I hear you're living in the back of that feed store." Mrs. Bartlett reached into her purple shirt to pull up lavender straps that had slipped onto her arms.

"Yes, that's where we live." She ignored the Isabel comment. "What are all these books for?" She picked up a thin one with a picture of Taggert Creek's park on the front.

"Just doing a little research, dearie. I'm president of the Historical Society, don't you know?"

Izzy didn't know, but she nodded anyway.

Mrs. Bartlett pulled a Kleenex from her purple purse and mopped her forehead. "I trust you have studied about our little town's history at school?"

"Not really," Izzy said.

Mrs. Bartlett propped both her hands on her very large hips and looked at Mrs. Webb, the librarian. "Did you hear that, Marion? What are they teaching our young people at that fancy school on the highway if they're not teaching about the very history they are benefiting from by living in Taggert Creek?" Mrs. Bartlett stopped to pull in air. "If you ever have any questions about our little town, Isabel Dunn, you just come see me, don't you know."

Sounded like boring stuff to Izzy.

Beeps sounded as Mrs. Webb scanned the numbers on the back of the books Mrs. Bartlett was checking in. "Did you find what you were looking for in these books, Myrtle?"

"Oh yes. The new ones you ordered from Topeka were just wonderful." She grabbed the book Izzy was holding. "Now, this one is my own personal copy. I brought it to read during my break, but I want you to take it home, Isabel." Mrs. Bartlett fanned herself with an envelope. "It's important to know your history, don't you know?"

Mrs. Bartlett sniffed, grabbed her purse, then waddled away.

Mrs. Webb grinned, "Isn't she something?" She pushed Mrs. Bartlett's book toward Izzy.

"I'm going to look around a little," Izzy said and picked up the book.

"Wonderful. You haven't checked anything out in a long time. There are some new mysteries you might like."

"Good, thanks."

An ache grew in Izzy's chest as she moved toward the shelves. A girl from Michael's class was in the children's section, reading to some little kids. The words of *Owl Moon* tugged at Izzy. When she was little, she pretended her daddy took her for a winter walk to hear the owls. She swallowed the tightness in her throat, then ran her fingers along the spines of books on the shelf. Miss Bertie's song started as a whisper.

"What'll I do when you are far away, hm-hm, hm-hm, hm..."

She closed her eyes and grabbed the side of the bookcase. She saw the alley and Cleopatra and a strange smile on the lips of an old woman. Izzy's eyes flew open when she felt a touch on her arm.

"Isabel?" Mrs. Webb's voice wavered like it was far away. "The song you were singing was beautiful, but it was a little loud."

"I'm sorry," Izzy mumbled and pushed the librarian's arm away. "I've got to go."

"No, I think you should wait a minute." Mrs. Webb put her finger under Izzy's chin and turned her face. "You are so pale." She guided her to a chair. "Let me get you a glass of water."

Izzy glanced at the big clock on the wall behind the shelved books. "No, I'm fine. I need to go." She ran from the library.

The hot wind toasted her face, and cicadas in the trees clicked even louder. She took the shortcut behind the laundry mat to the back of the theater. By the time she got to the rusted car, her head was pounding. When she leaned down to grab the plastic sack from the front seat of the old car, little points of light danced in front of her eyes. She stumbled into the shade of the building and shivered in a breath of wind. She longed to go back to the feed building and stretch out, but she forced herself to walk to the back door of the theater.

Gravel crunched under her sandals. One little push and sunshine poured in from behind. Her shadow stretched across the floor and into the flour still carefully spread on the wooden planks. Tiny cat prints were the only sign that it wasn't just as she'd left it.

"No human prints?" Izzy leaned against the doorframe, staring at the flour-dusted floor, trying to make sense of it.

"Meow."

She jumped when Cleopatra's hair brushed across her ankle. "Hey, pretty girl." Cleopatra pressed dainty paws in a new pattern through the flour. Izzy bent to pet her. A bump sounded in the theater, causing Cleopatra to bolt out the door. She streaked under the abandoned car. Izzy turned away from the sunshine and was reaching for the handle to pull the door shut when she noticed another difference.

Only cat prints were in the flour, but what was on the box left her breathless. The flowers were gone from the rusty can, and...

Beside the can.

On its side.

An *empty* cottage cheese container.

"How could someone get the cake without going through the flour?"

Izzy's breaths came in short gasps. Ghosts eat cake! She slid around the corner and through the alley like Dirty Bertie was right behind her.

What'll I do? hm-hmmm... The melody filled her head. *Hm-hm-hm...* It seemed to echo from the brick walls of the alley. *When I'm alone, hm-hmmm, hm-hm-hm-hmmm...* She stopped running and dropped under Bertie and Tom's brick. Eyes closed, she waited for her heart to stop hammering in her chest. She reached with shaking fingers to feel the roughness of the letters on the bricks—Bertie and Tom 1943.

Was it a younger version of Dirty Bertie who carved the words, or did she and Tom carve them together while sneaking a kiss in the alley? Izzy felt a blush spread over her cheeks. It suddenly felt wrong to call the old woman Dirty Bertie. Even if she was a ghost, Izzy somehow felt connected. She traced the names on the brick again.

"I'll call you Miss Bertie," she said.

It felt good.

Familiar.

Right.

CHAPTER 30

"Get out the sandwich stuff while I finish up this feed order," Mom said.

Izzy was glad for something else to think about besides tiny cat prints and ghosts eating cake. She pulled bologna, bread, and mustard from the refrigerator and put them on the table.

"How's our lunch coming?" Mom rubbed her hands together. "Looks good. I'll go wash my hands. Here's the key to the pop machine."

"Aren't Beth and Michael going to eat?"

Mom spoke over the running water in the bathroom, "No, I sent Michael to the sale barn to talk to them about advertising the store on the wall during their sales. He was real excited about it." She came from the bathroom, wiping her hands on a towel. "And remember Beth has that babysitting job for the rest of the day."

"Oh, yeah. I forgot." Izzy set two cans of pop on the table and stared at the mustard jar. "Did Maverick go with Michael?"

"You bet," Mom said. "They've become quite the buddies."

Picturing Maverick's head hanging out the window made Izzy smile. But, there was a lonely feeling too.

"Ding-ding."

"Oh, there's the door. I'll take my plate with me. Make sure you clean all this up when you finish." She pushed the swinging door with her hip while raising her Pepsi can to her lips.

Izzy wished mom had stayed. Maybe then she could quit thinking about the theater and the missing cake. She chewed her sandwich and frowned in deep thought. Suddenly, she dropped the sandwich and slapped her forehead.

It was so obvious.

"Cleopatra ate the cake. But what happened to the flowers? Maybe I didn't notice them on the floor."

She crammed the rest of her sandwich in her mouth and took gulps of her drink. Just before she pushed through the swinging door, she heard Mom.

"I've been really worried about Izzy. I hear her saying things in her sleep about the fire and the theater next door."

"I'll be glad to talk to her if you want me to." The voice sounded familiar, but it didn't matter. No way was Izzy going to talk to anyone about the fire. She gave the swinging door a push and opened her mouth to say she was going for a walk. Instead of words, a long, loud burp echoed from deep in her stomach. Izzy's hands flew to her mouth.

"Isabel!" Mom looked horrified.

The man, who stood with his back to Izzy, turned with a grin.

It was the preacher.

"Wow, Kiddo. That was a good one." He threw his head back and laughed. "You could win a contest. I burped *I Love You* to my wife when we were dating just to gross her out."

Izzy giggled but stopped when she saw Mom's face. "Excuse me. I...I guess I drank my pop too fast." Another giggle bubbled from her throat. "I'm going for a walk."

"Good idea." Mom's face was bright red. "Pastor Smith is checking on us." Mom ran her fingers through her hair.

Izzy smiled back at the minister then remembered the conversation she'd just overheard. "Nice to, uh, see you. I gotta go." She left the office like she was late for something. She didn't want to think about what questions he might ask about her *feelings*. What if God gave him special powers to pry the truth out of people? No. She couldn't take a chance on that.

She walked past the alley and glanced at the roof of the theater. Pigeon sounds floated down from the tower. She stepped into the street so she could see the birds on the roof. Her eyes followed the drips of bird poop that ran down from the vents to...

She shaded her eyes with her hand. Just below the tower was a row of windows from one end of the theater to the other. They always had shades pulled down. This time, something was different. She squinted to look at the window in the middle.

"What was that?" she whispered. A shadow? No a face—definitely a face. A shiver ran up her back. She stepped to the side of the street when Mrs. Bartlett drove by in her purple car. Izzy waved, then moved back where she could see the windows. Nothing.

"That face ate my cake. I know it."

Gravel crunched as Izzy pivoted and ran through the alley. Plowing through the weeds, she ignored Cleopatra, who held court on the car hood. A shove on the back door of the theater released white flour dust into the air.

And then she stopped.

"Wow!" Izzy held her breath while she tried to process the scene in front of her. The tomato can she'd rescued from the ground sat on the wooden box. But, instead of yellow flowers, it held a bouquet of iridescent peacock feathers. An eye-like design stared from each quill.

Izzy squatted when the cat rubbed against her leg. "What is all this, Cleopatra?" She reached for a folded piece of paper resting between the feathers and a dented metal flashlight. The paper was yellowed like old newspapers, and it crackled when Izzy opened it. The words were written with one of those fountain pens you had to fill with ink from a bottle.

Dear Little Girl,

Thank you for the lovely flowers and cake. I don't usually receive guests, but since you persist in coming to my theater uninvited, I might say, please introduce yourself like a proper young lady. Follow the hallway to the staircase. I'll be waiting.

Cordially yours,

Miss Bertie Gothard

"So now the ghost is writing letters?"

Izzy raised her hands to the top of her head. Bologna and cheese lay like a rock in her stomach.

Outside, in the alley, everything was normal.

Safe.

The sun glinted off something shiny on the old car, and butterflies flew from flower to flower through the weeds. Izzy raked her teeth over her bottom lip, back and forth. She wanted to run back to the store. She wanted to swing in the park with the wind blowing her hair. Anything but go down that hallway.

So...why did she pick up the flashlight?

CHAPTER 31

I t was like a crossroad where Izzy had to choose a direction. There was nothing smart about going into the dark building. She shook with the fear of it. But, she was more afraid not to go. The familiar song floated toward Izzy while she stood at the edge of the light.

"What'll I do when you are far away? Hm-hm-hm-hmmm..."

She closed her eyes and pressed her back against the wall. The metal flashlight felt cold in her hand when she flipped the switch. Taking stiff, shuffling steps into the darkness, her feet stirred up dust that flew into the beam of light. She raised the light and hesitated when she recognized the dinosaur shape on the ceiling, and then the pirate with his ugly sneer and blazing eyes.

"Argh. Ha, ha, ha."

Izzy's heart throbbed like a drum in her ears. "This is so stupid," she said in a whisper, then looked back where sunlight blazed through the open door.

Thump, thump, thump.

She turned her body toward the sound and away from the sunlight. Green animal eyes shone in the flashlight's beam.

"Meow."

"Cleopatra?" Izzy's voice wobbled.

Thump, thump, thump.

A silent scream stuck in her throat. The thumping continued, then stopped.

"Little girl, are you coming up to meet me, or should Cleopatra and I go back to our own business?"

The lady's voice sounded grumpy but didn't seem like someone who would murder her and bury her body under the theater floor. Izzy closed her mouth and swallowed, trying to make enough spit to un-dry her throat.

"I, I'm coming."

It wasn't the song or curiosity about the theater. It was something else—something she didn't understand. But she knew she couldn't go back.

Izzy turned the flashlight on the floor in front of her. Coldness soaked into her body, raising goose bumps on her arms. She shuffled until she came to some stairs. Raising the light, step by step, she jumped when an old woman's face was spotlighted. It was wrinkled with a roadmap of lines and was framed with white hair. The face had the bluest eyes Izzy had ever seen. They tugged at her heart with a familiarity she couldn't explain. She remembered the hand that reached toward her during the prayer at her dad's grave—the hand of this woman who signed her name, Bertie Gothard.

"Follow me," the woman said, then she turned and thumped up the stairs with her upside-down broom.

Cleopatra's thin body slipped between Izzy's feet and streaked past her. Izzy followed, wondering if the creaking steps were strong enough. The staircase curved in a spiral and finally ended at a bright red door that slammed shut. A large sign said, PRIVATE.

"Why would she invite me to visit and then slam the door?" Izzy asked Cleopatra. The cat stared and gave a soft meow. Either Miss Bertie was a ghost, or a crazy old lady like Michael said.

Both possibilities made Izzy's legs go weak.

A little girl's giggle floated from deep in the theater. More shivers and triple goose bumps. She bit her lip and knocked three times on the door.

"Yes, who is it, please?"

"Well, uh-hem, it's me, Izzy, I mean Isabel Dunn."

"Yes?"

"Uh, can I...I mean, may I come in?"

"Certainly, young lady." The thumping sound came closer. The door swung open, and the stairway was filled with light. "Do come in."

Izzy shaded her eyes against blinding sunshine. It was as if the red door had transported her to another time. The room was filled with high-back chairs and a sofa with claw feet. All the furniture had lacy cloths across the backs and the arms. In the middle of the room was a square table with the yellow weed bouquet Izzy had left on the wooden box. Cups and saucers were in front of two chairs.

Miss Bertie had been waiting for her.

CHAPTER 32

"Where are my manners? Won't you sit down?" the woman said. "I'll just check on our kettle for tea." She thump-shuffled into another room.

Izzy pulled out one of the chairs and sat with caution on the edge of the seat. Sun streamed through the windows, but a chill settled on her arms.

"What am I doing?" she said. Clouds covered the sun, and Izzy jumped when a crack of thunder rumbled across the sky outside. A teakettle whistled. She glanced toward the door.

"Here we are," the woman said as she thumped into the room. "I'm sorry, I don't have loose tea. It is so much better, but these tea bags will do."

She wore gloves as she poured water from a shiny kettle into each cup. A strange smell made Izzy's nose twitch.

"I trust you like Earl Grey tea. It is the only kind my family ever drinks." The lady set the kettle on a fancy potholder and dropped her body into the chair across from Izzy. She propped her broom against the wall. "Oh, I seem to have forgotten our cookies. Would you mind, dear? They are in the kitchen. You'll see them by the pie safe."

Izzy was glad to get up and shake out the wiggles. The room she entered was like a large closet. There was a deep metal sink, an ancient white stove with two burners, and what she guessed was a refrigerator. It looked like one she saw in the Kansas museum. Not sure what a pie safe was, she scanned the rest of the room and found a plate with the same round cookies the lady had left on the wooden box. She swallowed, feeling dryness in her throat.

"This is crazy!" She turned in a circle, searching for a back door.

"Did you find the cookies, dear?"

"Yes, I found them." Izzy took a deep breath. She carried the plate carefully to the table and sat across from Miss Bertie.

"Would you care for sugar in your tea? Of course, you would. One lump or two?"

"Uh...two, I guess," Izzy said, still planning an escape.

Miss Bertie reached some miniature tongs into a small round bowl and pulled out two square cubes. They looked like dice without the dots. She dropped them into Izzy's cup with a plop. She put one square in her own cup then used a spoon to stir. Izzy did the same but waited until Miss Bertie took the first sip.

After blowing on the hot liquid, the lady said, "Please, drink your tea, dear. Oh, and help yourself to a molasses cookie." She pushed the plate across the table and smiled. Her teeth were long and stained. "These are my grandmother's recipe.

Izzy took a cookie and set it on the saucer. She raised the cup to her lips and took a sip. "Mmmm," she said softly. It didn't taste like Grandma Dunn's tea, but it didn't taste like anything else she'd ever had either. "This is kinda good."

The skin around the woman's eyes crinkled when she smiled. Miss Bertie took another sip then set the cup in the saucer with a clink.

Her smile faded.

"Now, tell me why you persist in coming to my theater without an invitation, Miss Isabel."

Izzy's mouth dropped open. "How do you know my name?

Miss Bertie raised her eyebrows and looked over the top of her small glasses. "Oh, I hear so many things up in this old theater." She crossed her arms and set her mouth in a thin line. "Actually, you told me your name when I answered the door."

"Oh, right." Izzy took another sip.

"You haven't answered my question. Why would you want to come into this old building?"

The lady's voice was firm but didn't seem too scary. Izzy decided to tell the truth. After all, Mom was just a building away, and she knew she could outrun an old lady.

"Well, everyone says this theater is haunted. I heard you talk on the other side of the door one night when I took my dog for a walk." Izzy slurped her tea.

"Continue." Bertie's hand slowly moved the spoon in circles inside her cup.

"Well, I was just curious." Izzy's chair creaked as she squirmed. "My friend, Ariel, came with me when your cat ran into a hole in the wall. We wanted to see if the cat was okay."

"So what did you and your friend find?" The spoon was still moving in circles, round and round.

Izzy tried to swallow. "The first time we both ran when we saw the pirate. Then the next time, we got as far as the pirate again, but he started talking and his eyes. They were creepy. Just like today." She set her cup on the saucer and talked around the wad of cookie. "Why a pirate?"

"Ha-ha!" Miss Bertie clapped her hands. "That's Captain Crowbar. He's been a part of this theater ever since I can remember. Poppa bought him for the opening of a movie about Buccaneers and buried treasure." Her expression darkened. "The captain does a good job scaring off most intruders."

Izzy's throat was so dry the cookie choked her. She gulped the rest of the tea and hugged her shivering body. Miss Bertie silently watched. The woman looped her fingers together and tapped the sides of both index fingers against her lips.

Miss Bertie dropped her hands to her lap and stared into Izzy's eyes. "Tell me, dear, why were you crying in the doorway?"

Izzy turned toward the windows to avoid the woman's eyes. A pigeon sat on the windowsill, cooing. Innocent. Safe.

"I needed someplace to be alone." An urge to tell this woman the truth bubbled inside her. "It was my birthday, and I was sad because I thought Mom forgot." Izzy used her thumb to smash the cookie crumbs on the plate. "My friend Ariel couldn't come over and…and…" Izzy bent her head and pressed her palms between her knees. Her throat closed around the rest.

The dark shadow left Bertie's face, "Oh, my goodness. Was that cake from your birthday? Well, of course, it was. It was delicious." She took another sip from her cup. "So, was there a party?"

"No, Mom said we didn't have the money, since, Dad…" Izzy pushed her chair back and stood. She didn't like where the conversation was heading. "I need to go, Miss Bertie. Thank you for the tea and cookie, and you know, thank you for that day I was hiding." She cleared her throat.

Miss Bertie rose slowly. "I know about your father, dear. I understand what it is like to lose someone."

Izzy licked her lips, then rubbed them together and said, "I don't want to talk about any of that. I gotta go." She started for the door.

"Oh, my goodness. Of course." Miss Bertie reached for the broom. "Your mother will be concerned. Why don't you take another cookie with you?" Her hand shook when she held out the plate. Horrible scars peeked through a gap between her long sleeve and glove.

Izzy tried not to stare.

"Thank you," she said and slipped the cookie into her pocket. "Is it alright if I borrow your flashlight? It's kinda dark."

"Well, of course." Bertie thumped across the room. "I have several. Just leave it on the wooden box for the next time you visit." She opened her eyes wide. They were blue like the sky. "You will visit again, won't you?"

Izzy hesitated before she said, "Okay, if you want me to." She wondered what her friends would say if they knew. "I'm glad you're not a ghost." Her hand flew to her mouth. "I'm sorry. It's just my friends. They said you were, you know, a ghost. They called you Dirty Bertie." Hand up again.

Bertie's laugh made Izzy smile and cringe at the same time.

"What makes you think I'm *not* a ghost?" The woman's smile vanished, and she leaned in close to Izzy's face. Her breath was gross and made Izzy turn away.

"Don't tell anyone about our little visit. I like my privacy. Captain Crowbar usually keeps the riff-raff out, but once in a while," she hesitated, "some persist."

"Oh, sure. I won't tell anybody." Izzy flipped the switch on the flashlight and wondered if she could keep the promise. She worked her way down the steps but stopped halfway and asked, "Miss Bertie, who else lives here? I heard someone giggle before I knocked on your door."

Miss Bertie ignored her question and said, "Make sure I tell you next time about the boys who got into the projection booth." Bertie's eerie cackle caused Izzy to cringe. "I scared them pretty good. You make sure I tell you."

The red door slammed shut. Izzy stared then took cautious steps down the stairs. The unknown girl's giggle echoed. Closer this time. On her left.

Izzy's feet pounded.

Captain Crowbar croaked.

The floorboards creaked.

She dropped the flashlight on the box and grabbed the note and feathers. The only human prints left were the outline of flip-flops mixed with cat paws in the dust.

****

"I understand you said you went for a walk. I just need to know why you were gone so long. And where in the world did you get the feathers?" Mom held them to the light. "They're beautiful. I don't know anyone who raises peacocks in town."

"Well," Izzy licked her lips, "like I said, I went for a walk. You know while you were talking to the preacher."

"Isabel..." Mom put a hand on her hip and cocked her head to the side.

"Honest. I went for a walk, and I met this old lady."

"What old lady?"

"I don't know her whole name, but she needed me to carry some stuff for her." Izzy pictured the strange kitchen above the theater, and she touched the cookie in her pocket. "Then the lady wanted to fix me something to drink. You know, to thank me. We were talking, and I lost track of time. Sorry, Mom."

Izzy wrapped her arms around her mom's neck.

"Don't be buttering me up. What about the feathers?" Mom looked at them again.

"That lady gave them to me. Aren't they pretty?"

She hadn't really lied yet—just left out a few details. "She wants me to come back sometime." Izzy snapped her mouth shut before she said too much.

"Well, I guess it's okay. Just don't take off without me knowing where you're going. Where does this lady live? Maybe I know her."

"Not far. Not sure of the address." Izzy reached to scratch mosquito bites on her legs.

"Quit scratching. They'll get infected." Mom looked at an envelope in her hand. "I need you to run this to the post office before it closes."

Izzy grabbed the envelope and bolted through the door before Mom could ask any more questions. She stepped off the sidewalk to see the windows of the theater's upstairs rooms. Miss Bertie stood in the center one. She raised her finger to her lips then pulled the shade down. The hairs raised on the back of Izzy's neck. She remembered the woman's words.

"What makes you think I'm *not* a ghost?"

CHAPTER 33

A week had crawled by since Miss Bertie's tea and cookies. Izzy checked the back door every day. It was always locked. If it hadn't been for the note hidden in her spiral and the peacock feathers by her bed, she could have convinced herself she imagined the whole thing.

She kind of wished she had.

Izzy counted the fifty-eight steps through the alley on her way to another book-less library visit. She almost walked past the open back door until a sound made her look back. Sunlight spotlighted the hall's wood floor.

"Meow."

"Cleopatra." Izzy stooped to run her hand along the cat's back. "Where have you been for so long?" The cat sprinted through the door, then doubled back to stare into Izzy's eyes.

Izzy bit into her thumbnail.

Took a deep breath.

Took the flashlight from the overturned box.

Followed the cat into the dark hallway, past the dinosaur shape on the ceiling.

"Argh. Ha, ha, ha." The captain's laugh vibrated off the walls.

Izzy double-timed past the spot where she heard the little girl giggle—thankful there was only the squeak of old boards under her feet.

Up the winding stairs.

Three knocks on the red door.

"Miss Bertie, it's me, Izzy." She jumped back when the door flew open.

"Isabel, dear. I was beginning to think you would never visit us again."

Izzy hated that name, but somehow, it sounded beautiful when Miss Bertie said it. She followed the old woman into the room, where the spicy smell of Earl Grey tea floated in the air. She wanted to remind the old woman the door had been locked, but Miss Bertie thumped into the little kitchen. She returned carrying a cake and a big smile.

"I am delighted for you to try my applesauce cake. It is an old family recipe that we only make on special occasions." She set the cake in the middle of the table. "Please, have a seat, dear. Could you pour the tea while I slice the cake?"

Izzy's hand shook while she poured the steaming liquid.

How did Miss Bertie know she was coming?

Izzy scooted her chair closer to the table, then forked a small bite of cake.

"Mmmm. This is good." It reminded her of the cookies Miss Bertie made, but the cake was sweeter with raisins and had white frosting. "Why is this a special occasion?"

"To celebrate your birthday, of course," Miss Bertie said. "And that's not all, Isabel. I have a gift for you." Miss Bertie leaned in and said in a breathy voice, "I'm going to share a secret." She sat back in her chair and took a sip of tea. "No doubt you have seen the brick with my name on it in the alley."

Izzy nodded then said, "The one under the window?"

"Yes, now here is the secret." She leaned in again and said.

"Three bricks to the left,

with both hands strong,

push in and wait.

Your secrets belong."

Miss Bertie took another sip and pulled a paper from her pocket. I've written it down for you."

"Uh, thank you." Izzy took the piece of crinkly paper. "What secrets?"

"The ones you write down, of course. We can't let anyone else read them, can we?"

Izzy felt cold and hot at the same time. "How did you know I write things down?"

Miss Bertie ignored her question. "Finish your cake, dear, and drink your tea before it gets cold."

Izzy bit the inside of her cheek.

The old clock ticked on the wall.

Cleopatra purred near Miss Bertie's feet.

Izzy searched for something to fill the silence.

She took a sip of tea then said, "You told me to remind you about some boys who sneaked into the theater."

Staring at Izzy with blank eyes, the old woman said, "Oh, yes. I remember." She poured more tea. "Young people often dare one another to come sneaking into the theater." She raised her cup to her lips and sipped. "They are just sure it is haunted. I can usually scare them off by pounding my broom on the floor—and then, of course, there's Captain Crowbar." She set her cup onto the saucer with a clink and laughed with a dry crackling sound that made Izzy glad there was sunlight pouring in the windows instead of moonlight.

"Why do you carry the broom?" That seemed like a safe question. "Why not a cane?"

Again, there was a blank stare. "That's a good question, but it's been so long. Oh yes. I remember. Years ago, I twisted my ankle. The broom worked pretty well, so I just kept using it." Her eyes crinkled. "Besides, it adds to the mystery, don't you think?"

Izzy nodded, remembering her dad's funeral and Miss Bertie holding the broom.

"Well, back to my story. When I heard those boys in the projection room, I knew they were up to no good, so I slipped up the back way and listened." She let her voice drop to a whisper. "They were trying to figure out the projector. They got it going long enough for the last cartoon we showed to flicker on the screen." She looked toward the ceiling. "I think it was about a cat."

Cleopatra jumped onto Miss Bertie's lap. "Oh, not about you, precious—not nearly as beautiful as you." She stroked the cat, and Cleopatra arched her back, enjoying the attention.

"So, what happened?"

"What happened to what, dear?" Another blank stare. "Oh, of course. Well, that projector had been left to dust for so long, it soon started smoking. That's when I pounded my broom and screeched."

"Eeeeckkk!"

Izzy slapped her hands over her ears and screamed a little herself. "You should have seen them run."

A nervous laugh slipped through Izzy's lips. She pushed her chair back a little. But her curiosity made her ask. "What about the projector? Is it still there?"

"Rest assured, it is still there," Bertie said. "I pulled the plug, and the smoke stopped." Her face grew dark. "I could have lost *everything*."

Izzy gripped the sides of her chair and tried to think of another subject to pull Bertie from whatever scary thoughts she was having. "Why don't you live in a house?" She glanced around the room filled with furniture. "I mean, this is nice, but…"

The old woman stood with her back stiff. "It's time for you to leave." She grabbed the broom and thumped to the door.

"I'm sorry. Did I say something wrong?" Izzy passed through the red door and turned to face Miss Bertie.

She wouldn't look directly at Izzy but pushed the flashlight toward her with shaky gloved hands. "Be careful on the steps, Isabel."

The door shut with a thud.

Izzy shouted through the red door, "I'm sorry." She held her breath and waited for Miss Bertie to change her mind. All she heard was the thumping broom and the door to another room slamming shut.

"Fine." Izzy hurried down the steps. "I don't know why you're so mad," she mumbled. "I'm the one who comes up here in the dark and drinks that weird tea. Just see if I come back."

She halted and shouted up the stairs, "And my name is IZZY!"

Organ music boomed from deep in the theater. Izzy twisted in a circle and whipped her head toward the sound. She recognized the wedding march from an old movie, but the notes were so much darker. The melody swelled until the walls rattled with it. Down the long hall, sunshine spilled onto the floor of the open door. Heart pounding, Izzy ran to the exit and slammed the door behind her. It sounded like every door in the building slammed with it

One.

After.

The other.

CHAPTER 34

eth leaned over Izzy's shoulder and said, "Don't forget to dust the bottles."

"You're not my boss," Izzy muttered. But she kept working. Sad. She had nothing better to do than dust bottles of insect spray. The last row was finished when Mom pushed through the office door.

"How did things go while I was gone?" Mom was smiling, but her eyes looked sad.

"Good," Beth answered. "Izzy is dusting, and I sold two bags of chicken feed."

"*We* sold two bags of chicken feed," Izzy said.

"What do you mean, *we*? You didn't do anything."

"Did too. I opened..."

"Girls! That's enough. It doesn't matter who sold the feed." Mom turned. "Izzy, are you finished with this book? I found it under some papers when I was cleaning off my desk this morning? It's not over-due, is it?" She flipped the book to the cover with a picture of old downtown Taggert Creek. "Why did you check this out anyway?"

Izzy took it from her. "I didn't. Mrs. Bartlett wanted me to read it. She got all mad that I didn't know much about Taggert Creek's history. I took it just so she would stop talking. Looks boring to me." She fanned the pages and noticed the book had pictures.

"Well, if you're not going to read it, take it back. We barely have enough money to buy toilet paper, let alone replace an expensive book like that." Mom went into the back room.

Izzy skimmed the pages again to find the faded picture of what looked like Miss Bertie's theater. She could feel Beth's eyes.

"That's it!" she said to herself. It was the same building, but the tower was half-built. Men stood on the roof with tools. She battled to keep her eyes on the picture without reading the words.

"I'm going across the street to the park. Okay, Mom?" She wanted to study the picture without Beth being nosy.

Mom hollered from the back rooms, "That's fine. Water the flowers out front before you go."

Watering the flowers in the barrel was one of Izzy's favorite chores, but that day she just dumped the water in one swoosh and dropped the can on the pavement. She ran across the street to a picnic bench and faced the front of the theater. She stared at the front cover. It wasn't the kind of book she'd ever get from the library.

But...

It was the kind she would use for a report.

"So if this is like a school project, that would make reading okay," she said to herself. It was as if she'd been freed from prison. She opened the book and devoured the words.

"1927 - Workers add a tower to the top of Gothard's Theater," she read out loud.

First a community building and city hall. Then someone named Abner Gothard bought it from Taggert Creek and made it into a theater.

151

"I bet that's Miss Bertie's father." Izzy glanced at the old building. She turned the page and saw a picture of a white house with some castle-like towers in the corners. Below it was the same house with flames shooting from the roof.

"Abner Gothard's home burned on Christmas Eve, 1944," Izzy read in a whisper. Her arms tingled.

"Mr. Gothard, his wife, Esther, and their daughter's fiancé, Tom Griffin, were all overcome in the blaze."

Izzy raised her eyes to focus on the theater across the street. Miss Bertie's face was framed in the left window. It was like she was waiting for Izzy to read the words.

Like she wanted her to know.

"That's why you didn't want to talk about your house." Izzy's words so soft, even the wind couldn't have heard.

Slowly the old woman's head nodded.

The window blind closed like a curtain in a play.

"You lost everything," Izzy said.

Just.

Like.

Me.

CHAPTER 35

"Call Mrs. Bartlett, please, Mom." Izzy turned to inside the front cover of the book. "See. Here's her phone number."

"I will, just as soon as I finish with this invoice." Mom glanced over her shoulder. "You can clean the bathroom for me while you wait if you want."

Izzy didn't want to clean the bathroom. She wanted to go right now and ask about the theater.

And the fire.

And...

Too scary to think about other questions swimming in her brain.

Mom was putting the portable phone in its cradle when Izzy came back to the office, wiping her wet hands on her t-shirt.

"Mrs. Bartlett said you're welcome to go see her any time." Mom smiled. "Gets pretty excited about Taggert Creek, doesn't she?"

"Alright!" Izzy reached over the counter and gave Mom a big kiss on the cheek.

"She said to bring the book with you." Mom cocked her head and looked over the top of her glasses. "Why the sudden interest in *boring* history?"

"I don't know. It's just important to know it—don't you think?"

Mom looked doubtful.

Beth grunted.

Izzy grabbed the book and her sunflower spiral.

"Be back by supper," Mom called.

Izzy counted her steps through the park, over the railroad tracks, and down the hill to Mrs. Bartlett's little house. She slowed to a walk when she breathed in a sweet smell—like someone had sprayed the air with perfume. The yard in front of Mrs. Bartlett's house was filled with a lavender glow of purple flowers on tall bushes. She walked to the door, ready to press the bell when it flew open.

"Isabel, hello! Come in, come in." Izzy ignored the name. Mrs. Bartlett led her through the entryway to a room that exploded with flowers, ribbons, and PURPLE.

"Wow!" Izzy said.

"Isn't it beautiful? I had the sofa recovered, and I just love it." Izzy coughed to keep from laughing.

"Now," Mrs. Bartlett said, "tell me what you thought of the book." She sat on her newly covered purple sofa and motioned toward the chair across from her.

"Well, I didn't read all of it but I did see the part about the old theater," Izzy said. She sat on the edge of the chair. "You know, the one beside our store. You're such an expert, I thought maybe I could ask you some questions."

Mrs. Bartlett fiddled with the beads on her necklace. "Well, I don't know about being an expert, but I do happen to know quite a bit about that place." She patted the sofa beside her. "Why don't you bring that book over here and tell me what you already know?"

Afternoon light crept across the floor while they looked at black and white pictures and old newspaper clippings. Izzy made a list of notes in her sunflower notebook.

"I was just a little girl when the Gothard house burned, but I'll never forget seeing those flames on Christmas Eve," Mrs. Bartlett said.

Izzy felt an ache begin in her chest. Miss Bertie wasn't angry when Izzy asked why she didn't live in a house—she was hurting.

Izzy turned away.

"Now, don't be ashamed of how you feel." Mrs. Bartlett handed her a lavender tissue. "You and Bertie have a lot in common. You both lost everything, don't you know?" She took Izzy's hand and patted it. "Bertie's fiancé, Tom, was very handsome in his uniform." The woman's cheeks glowed pink. "I admit I had a crush on him."

Izzy smiled and tried to picture Mrs. Bartlett as a little girl in a purple dress.

"Bertie and her parents were so good to me." She sniffed. "It about broke my heart when my parents told me they were all dead."

Izzy stood and crossed to the window. She watched bumblebees slip in and out of tiny blossoms. Their buzzing so loud, she could hear it through the glass. She and Miss Bertie did have a lot in common, but not everything. It wasn't Miss Bertie's fault her beautiful house burned and her father died. Izzy tugged on the neck of her t-shirt like she was suffocating. She wanted to run from the buzzing purple world, but she had one more question.

Her voice bounced off the glass of the window, "What happened to her?" She turned to see Mrs. Bartlett's lips pressed together. "What happened to Miss Bertie?"

"Oh, there were countless rumors about her. None of them true, don't you know?" Mrs. Bartlett heaved herself from the couch and stood beside Izzy at the window.

"What are the rumors?" Izzy asked.

"Oh...some say she died in the fire, and her body was never found. Others say she ran away and died in a mental hospital in Topeka. But, none of that is true." Mrs. Bartlett turned on the ceiling fan.

"What do *you* think happened?" Izzy asked.

"I know part of it because she came to our house that night. It's not a pretty story." Mrs. Bartlett left the room and came back with a picture in an old metal frame. She handed it to Izzy. "This is how I'd like to remember them." It was a black and white photo of a soldier and a woman with familiar eyes.

"This is Bertie Gothard?" asked Izzy.

"Yes." She took the picture back and sighed. "It was their engagement photograph. Bertie gave this copy to my parents, or it would have been destroyed in the fire.

Mrs. Bartlett set the frame on the coffee table like it was precious. "Bertie was burned terribly on her arms and hands. Momma tried to keep me in my room so I wouldn't see it, but I sneaked out while the doctor did what he could." She stopped talking to blow her nose. "Bertie wouldn't say a word. She stared straight ahead like she didn't see anyone. She kept humming a song that has stayed with me all these years. I found a recording of it. Would you like to hear it?"

"Yes," Izzy said louder than she intended. Mrs. Bartlett went to a large wooden cabinet. There was an electric snap when she turned on the power. Then a static clicking before the melody floated across the room and mingled in Izzy's mind with the version she'd heard Miss Bertie humming in the theater.

"After she recovered from her burns, she moved into an apartment above the theater." Mrs. Bartlett sighed and stacked some papers. "I never saw her again. She became a recluse, probably because of the scars."

Izzy thought of the long sleeves that covered Miss Bertie's arms and the gloves she always wore. "What happened to her after that?" she whispered.

"Now, Isabel," Mrs. Bartlett looked at her over the top of her glasses and smiled, "I'm sure you've heard the rumors that she haunts that old theater."

Izzy opened her mouth to say Miss Bertie was alive in the theater now. But then she remembered her friend's face and the gloved finger to her lips. Izzy had promised to guard the secret.

"Thank you." Izzy stood and hugged her notebook to her chest. "Mom said to be back by supper. I better go."

Mrs. Bartlett pulled herself from the couch. "Well, of course, dear. I'm glad you came. I hope you'll visit again." She opened the front door.

"Thank you, I will." Izzy started down the sidewalk.

"Before you go, I want to ask you something." Mrs. Bartlett's thick shoes made a squeaking noise as she walked toward Izzy.

"Why are you so interested in the theater? It doesn't seem like something a young girl would think much about." The sun winked off her glasses.

She had to think fast. Miss Bertie made her promise. "Well, I thought I would start working on a report for school about Taggert

Creek. You know, so other kids will know about our history—like you said."

Adults love it when you talk about schoolwork.

Mrs. Bartlett kind of puffed up like birds do in the winter. "Well, now. I think that is just marvelous."

Izzy walked past the lilac bushes then stopped. "Would you mind if I picked some of these flowers for my mom? She loves how they smell."

"The lilacs? Well, of course. I wish I'd thought of it." She went into the house and brought back a pair of scissors and a paper sack. Honeybees scattered as she snipped several clusters of the purple flowers and dropped them in the sack.

"There you go. You tell your mom I said hi." She wiped her forehead with a tissue.

Izzy pushed her face into the sack and said, "Hmmmmm." Mrs. Bartlett smiled so big her cheeks made her eyes crinkle into tiny slits.

"I'm sorry to keep bothering you, but just one more question," Izzy said. "Where was Miss Bertie's house, the one that burned?" she asked.

Mrs. Bartlett's forehead wrinkled. "I thought I told you. It was right there." She pointed behind Izzy. "Across the street, on the corner. Such a beautiful place. I don't know who owns the property, but I make sure it is mowed." She pointed. "You can still see the rock wall and stone steps from the front of the house."

Izzy walked backward toward the street. "Thanks again, Mrs. Bartlett, for everything."

"My pleasure. You come back anytime."

Izzy took her time getting to the corner then turned back to make sure Mrs. Bartlett had gone into her house. She wanted to be alone when she sat on Miss Bertie's steps.

The steps where her friend lost everything too.

CHAPTER 36

A hot wind meandered through Taggert Creek, causing farmers to search for shade. The wind rustled the leaves of the ancient trees above the girl's head, but her only thoughts were of a long-gone white house and the fire that destroyed it.

Fifty-nine, sixty, sixty-one steps and her toes were touching the ruins of Miss Bertie's house.

Izzy closed her eyes, head back. It must have been beautiful. She bent to touch the huge slabs of pink rock with silvery sparkles. Sitting on the lowest one, not caring if anyone was watching, she laid her face and arms across the step above her. The rock was cool in comparison to the blistering wind. She imagined sitting on the porch, drinking Earl Grey tea with Miss Bertie Gothard. And her Tom.

"Hm-hm-hm-hmmm, hm-hm-hm." The notes of the song vibrated in the stone under her ear. She sat straight up. There was nothing around her except the grass and the trees bending. "Hm-hm-hm-hmmm." She stood and turned in all directions. The skin on the back of her neck tingled. But, instead of running, she sat back with her hands pressed against the rock.

"What'll I do when you are far away, and I'm so blue, what'll I do?"

The song filled her, no longer with fear or loneliness, but with...a settled feeling. Nothing else mattered.

****

Time might have stopped or an hour might have passed. Izzy wasn't sure. She backed from the rock steps, grabbed the sack of flowers and notebook, and ran toward the feed store. Mom would be worrying, but there was one place she had to go first.

Sweat soaked through her shirt by the time Izzy slid to a stop behind the theater. Inside the back door, she grabbed the rusty soup can from the wooden box and filled it with water from the faucet. After arranging half the lilacs in the can, she tore paper from her spiral and wrote a note. Her hands shook so much she had to stop and start over. Twice.

Dear Miss Bertie,
Sorry I said something wrong.
I think I understand now.
Please, I need to talk to you.
Isabel

She set the can of flowers on the edge of the paper and pulled the door back the way she'd found it. In the alley, she stopped across from the Bertie and Tom brick.

Miss Bertie was right. It was time to hide the spiral. She pulled out the poem Miss Bertie had given her.

"Three bricks to the left,
with both hands strong,
push in and wait.
Your secrets belong."

She looked at the poem again to memorize it, then stuffed the paper in the spiral and dropped the notebook at her feet. Glancing to both ends of the alley to make sure no one was coming, she counted to the left.

"One, two, three." She stood on tiptoes and pushed with both hands. There was a grinding sound, and a metal drawer with the brick cover jutted from the building.

"Wow!"

She grabbed her spiral and set it carefully in the drawer. It was a perfect fit. The poem didn't say how to shut it, so she pushed on the brick with both hands again. The brick drawer slowly went back in place with a gritty screech.

"No one will find it now." She just hoped it would open when she needed it.

****

"Izzy, these are beautiful." Mom put the lilacs in a jar and set them on the folding table in the kitchen. "I'll have to call Mrs. Bartlett and thank her."

Izzy hadn't thought about that.

Michael filled his plate with spaghetti and salad. Suppers were better since someone gave mom an old stove with two electric burners and a small oven.

"Hey, Squirt, it's against the law to steal flowers from someone's yard, isn't it?" He threw his leg over and around the back of his chair and sat.

Beth stuck her nose into the flowers and said, "Ummmm. They do smell good."

"I didn't steal them, Michael," Izzy said, then dished spaghetti onto her plate. "And it ought to be against the law to take more than your share of the spaghetti."

Mom rubbed her hand on Izzy's back. "Let's not start arguing about the food. There's plenty."

Izzy took her plate to the table and asked, "Mom, have you ever been inside Mrs. Bartlett's house? It's like a grape explosion."

Mom wiped her mouth on a paper towel. "No, I haven't, but I'm not surprised." She swallowed then said, "She's been addicted to purple since I can remember."

They all laughed, and it felt nice.

Mom cleared her throat and changed the subject. "So, tell me. What's the real reason you wanted to spend a summer afternoon talking to Mrs. Bartlett about history?"

Uh-oh.

"Umm…I'm…gonna write a report. I'm sure my teachers next year will want to see it." She shoveled the last of her spaghetti into her mouth so she wouldn't have to answer any more questions for a while.

"Yeah, right," Michael said, then he burped. The bell on the front door jingled.

"Michael, didn't you lock the door when you came in?" Mom started to get up, but Michael stopped her.

"Sorry, Mom. I'll get it."

She shook her head and said, "You girls have got to be careful about locking that door when the office is closed. It's just not safe."

Izzy took a breath to remind her that Michael was the one who left it unlocked. Michael hollered before she could get the words out.

"Isabel, get out here."

She pushed through the swinging door, ready to explode about Michael using that name, but she stopped. He was locking the front door and shutting the blinds. When he turned, his face was pasty white.

"What's wrong? You look like you saw a…" The words stuck in Izzy's throat when she saw the note in his hand.

"Michael, where did you get that?"

"I told you not to go in that theater. I told you. Didn't I tell you?" Sweat beaded on his upper lip, and his eyes were wild.

"I didn't…"

"Don't try to lie your way out of this one." Michael's voice squeaked. "That crazy lady or ghost or whatever she is was just here. She was *here* in the store. She left you this note."

"How do you know who she…?" Izzy licked her dry lips while her brain whirred. "Michael," she whispered, "the projector. You were one of the boys who turned on the projector, weren't you?" An icy chill raced through her body.

Michael pushed past her and said, "Don't know what you're talking about." He shoved the swinging door open but came back and hissed just inches from her face. "You say one word about that to Mom or anyone else, and I'll…"

"I won't tell," she said.

"Well, if you do," he lowered his voice to a whisper right by her ear, "I think she'll find it very interesting that you've been sneaking into the theater and spending time with that loony old lady." He turned and strutted through the swinging door.

Izzy stared at the envelope in her hand, trying to think through what had just happened. Double blackmail.

Michael wouldn't tell.

Neither would she.

She looked down at the note. The paper crackled when she unfolded it.

Dear Isabel,

Thank you so very much for the lovely flowers. It has been many years since lilacs have graced my table. I remember when I was a girl, the family across the street had a yard full of the glorious blooms.

Izzy looked away from the paper and pictured Miss Bertie and her handsome soldier walking across the street. Miss Bertie pressing her nose against the blossoms. The smile.

I have no doubt you will visit me again.

Come when the moon is full of amber light,

and the wind is whispering your name.

Miss Bertha Gothard

Izzy slipped the note into her pocket. She grabbed the leash.

"Maverick needs to go out, Mom. I'll be right back."

She didn't wait for permission.

Maverick sniffed every crack in the alley pavement.

Izzy could only think of Miss Bertie.

She had to tell the old woman she understood. To confess her own guilt she was tired of carrying alone.

But the confession would have to wait.

The back door was locked tight.

CHAPTER 37

"Beth, how do you know when the moon's full?"

"You look outside after dark," she said. The bunks shimmied when Beth flopped onto her side.

"I *know* you can look outside, but isn't there some kind of way to know when it's going to be full before it happens?"

Beth's muffled voice sounded sleepy. "I don't know. I think calendars show it. Why? You thinking about becoming a werewolf or something?"

"No, just thinking," Izzy said.

The bed shook again. "Well, think without talking. I'm going to sleep."

Izzy ached to talk to someone about Miss Bertie's strange message, but Beth wasn't a good prospect.

Maybe Michael. He already knew about the theater.

Nope. Sure to freak out even more.

Mom?

No way. She knew she'd say too much and would end up with a lifetime grounding.

Izzy waited for Beth's soft snore, then slid off the side of the bed and dropped to the floor. Michael's light was out, and Mom's mouth

166

hung open with her glasses crooked across her closed eyes. A magazine across her chest.

Izzy pushed through the swinging door, trying to avoid the grating squeak it usually made. In the office, the streetlight threw strips of light through the blinds. She pulled back the edge to look for the moon but instead saw lightning flashing through the clouds. Rain pelted the flowers in the barrel on the sidewalk.

Maverick sat up with a jerk.

"Hey, boy. Thunder scare you?" Izzy plopped down beside him and he pushed his head under her arm, forcing a hug. She rubbed his ears and buried her face in his fur.

"I bet you miss him, don't you?" Maverick whined and licked Izzy's cheek.

She missed Dad too, but not the way you're supposed to. She'd always thought if she could keep from bugging him so much, things would get better. Hoped he'd love her the way he used to. Now, it would never happen. The weight of it made her chest hurt.

Izzy squeezed Maverick tight. "I'm sorry, boy." She leaned down to whisper in the dog's ear. "The fire. It was my fault." Her breath snagged in her throat.

"And you're the only one I can tell."

CHAPTER 38

No friends.

No unlocked theater door.

And every day even more boring than the one before it.

Izzy had even begun a "Boring Things About My Summer" list on a piece of computer paper—her spiral still in its hiding spot. The most exciting thing that happened all week was getting two postcards from Ariel.

"That's nice," Mom said when she handed Izzy the cards. One had a picture of a gorilla from the Omaha Zoo and the other a field of sunflowers. "What did she say?" Mom asked.

"Says she misses me. Woopie." Izzy dropped onto the couch.

"I don't know what to tell you. She won't be gone forever." Mom slipped some papers under the edge of the stapler and slammed her hand on it several times like she was trying to kill it. "Why don't you go to the library? You like that."

"I guess," Izzy said. She picked at her fingernails, remembering how good it felt to bring home a stack of books. "I guess that's what I'll do." She stood and sighed. "At least it'll be cooler."

The sun was already sizzling, and heat waves shimmered off the sidewalk in the distance. Someone had put a big banner in the park to advertise Taggert Creek's Street Fair on Founder's Day in June. It was the biggest thing that happened in Taggert Creek all year. Farmers from all over Kansas came because of the tractor pull alone.

The thought of having the celebration in the park across the street made Izzy smile. If only Ariel was back from Nebraska.

She jiggled the back door of the theater, not surprised it was still locked. Her fingers touched Miss Bertie's last note she kept in her pocket.

"Come when the moon is full with amber light."

Izzy was still clueless about how to find out when the next full moon was. None of their calendars had phases of the moon, and she was afraid to do a search on Mom's computer. You can only fake writing reports in the summer so many times.

"How am I supposed to know when to come to see you, Miss Bertie?" She picked up a handful of small rocks and started pitching them at the wooden fence nearby. Three tosses later, she dropped the rocks and slapped her forehead.

"Duh! How dumb am I?"

She retrieved her spiral from the brick drawer, then jumped through the weeds behind the laundry mat and raced to the library.

Icy air quickly cooled the sweat running down her back and made her shiver when she walked through the glass doors. Mrs. Webb was talking with someone but waved and winked. Izzy went straight to the computers in the center of the library and slipped into an empty spot. She pulled up the Internet but hesitated when she remembered her "no read" punishment.

"Educational. The moon is educational," she whispered to herself.

There were over a million hits about the moon. The pages about men walking on it caught her attention. She wondered what it would have been like to look at the moon and know that men were up there collecting rocks and hitting golf balls.

"So, Miss Isabel," Mrs. Webb said, "what's your search about today?"

Izzy winced at the name.

"The moon," she said.

Mrs. Webb sat in the empty chair beside Izzy's computer. "The moon? Hmmm. That's an interesting topic. What exactly do you want to know about the moon?"

Izzy took a breath and blew it out. "I want to know when it's full," she said. "You know when you can see all of it." She swallowed the tightness in her throat. "All I'm getting is a bunch of science stuff."

"Well, let's refine your search a little." Mrs. Webb typed in *phases of the moon* and hit the enter key. "There you go."

"Cool! Thanks." Izzy clicked on one of the pages. "Look. It shows how the moon changes every month. That's exactly what I wanted."

"Good. You let me know if you need anything else." She patted Izzy on the back and left.

Izzy started listing the moon's phases in her spiral—waxing crescent, waning crescent, full moon. Then she found a moon calendar.

She groaned when she saw the date for May. "Oh, I missed it," she said. Scrolling on to June, she smiled. "Perfect," she said and wrote in huge block letters in her notes.

FULL MOON, JUNE 7.

"Thanks, Mrs. Webb," she called then ran all the way back to the store.

"Mom!" Izzy burst through the office door.

Mom was on the phone and held up her hand. "Yes, yes. That sounds wonderful. They'll be excited too. Yes, Izzy's right here." She handed Izzy the phone.

"Who is it?" Izzy took the phone and said, "Hello?"

"Hey, Kiddo. How's my favorite twelve-year-old?"

"Grandpa! Hi." Izzy wiped the sweat from her forehead with her arm. "When are you coming to see us?"

"Next weekend for Founder's Day. How's that sound?" His voice made her smile.

"Awesome. Can't wait."

"Let me talk to your momma, and she can tell you the rest. Love you, kiddo," his voice wobbled.

"Love you too. Here's Mom."

She ran to tell Michael, but he drove away with Maverick before she could stop him. She looked up and down the street then hid the spiral in its secret place in the alley. Seeing the Founder's Day banner in the park across the street gave her excited tingles.

Then she remembered.

"Oh, my gosh!" Her hands flew to the top of her head. The excited tingles turned into panic.

"June 7th! The full moon."

CHAPTER 39

F lags snapped, engines roared from the rides in the park, the aroma of BBQ & popcorn floated in the breeze, and you could almost taste the excitement. It didn't take a calendar to realize there was a celebration in Taggert Creek.

"Are these enough pickles in the potato salad, Grandma?" Izzy slipped one into her mouth. The sweet and sour made her pucker.

"Let's see." Grandma Dunn wiped her hand on a towel and peeked over Izzy's shoulder. "Just perfect."

Izzy smiled and glanced at Beth, who was frosting the cake Grandma helped her bake. The feed store was closed for the holiday, and Mom had been banished to the motel room Grandma and Grandpa rented.

"You can sleep, watch TV, take a bubble bath, or whatever you want," they told her. Mom tried to argue, but they insisted.

Then they put the kids to work.

"OK, I'll finish that salad. You go check on your grandpa and Michael." She winked. "Make sure they haven't broken into the ice cream."

Izzy skipped from the office to the shady spot where Grandpa and Michael were working on homemade ice cream. She bent to pet Maverick, then leaned against Grandpa in a lawn chair.

"Grandma wants to know if it's done yet."

Grandpa sat back with his hands behind his head. "Well, Kiddo, as much as ol' Michael here is sweating, I'd bet it's getting close." He smiled and winked. "So, Michael, you ready for me to finish it up?"

"No way. I need the twenty bucks." Michael turned the handle a little faster making his face even redder. The ice crunched between the outside wooden bucket and the metal container on the inside.

"He's paying you to turn that handle?" Izzy asked.

Michael stopped turning and wiped his forehead with his sleeve. "Nope, he bet me I couldn't finish cranking it without his help." Michael blew his hair out of his eyes and went back to turning the handle. Grandpa winked again and added more ice chunks and rock salt inside the wooden bucket.

"You're pretty smart, Grandpa," Izzy whispered.

"Your daddy used to fall for the same trick," he said. Then he looked at Michael and stood. Izzy didn't know what to say while her grandpa looked off in the distance. She never realized how much Michael looked like him—Dad too. She felt a coldness in her stomach. Dad should have been there laughing at Michael. It would have been one of his happy days. Izzy turned with her head down.

Joy was gone.

Ugliness rushed in like someone turned on a faucet.

Grandpa cleared his throat. "Did your grandma send you out here to make sure we weren't doing a little taste test?"

She nodded, unable to squeeze out words.

"You women better bring out something to put the paddles in, or we just may have to start eating it right here before it melts."

She nodded again, then ran past the office door, the feed storage building, and into the alley. There was no breeze, only intense sunlight cooking the canyon. She leaned against the bricks, needing to feel the pain of their heat through her shirt. The carved names shone below the theater window across from her. Izzy stood and traced the words.

BERTIE AND TOM 1943

She imagined a beautiful young woman sitting under one of the big trees in front of the house from the picture. A soldier with his hat on his chest and his head across her lap smiled up at the younger version of Miss Bertie.

"Meow. Meow." Fur tickled against Izzy's legs.

"Cleopatra." Izzy bent to pick her up, but she streaked away before Izzy's fingers touched her fur.

"Wait. Come back."

Izzy slid around the corner just in time to see Cleopatra's body slip through the barely opened back door.

Open door!

Thrilled to find it unlocked after weeks, she pushed it open. The gritty sound of the door dragging on the floor felt familiar, nice. Sunshine shone on the wooden box, and the rusty tomato can now filled with white flowers. Grandma called them Queen Anne's Lace when they'd found the same kind growing in the ditch. Izzy touched the dainty lace-like blossoms and dropped her head to breathe them in. Weird. Smells like carrots.

A note slipped onto the dusty floor. Izzy's stomach flipped.

Dear Isabel,
When the moon is full with amber light,

And the wind is whispering your name,
Truth revealed with second sight,
No one left to blame.
Miss Bertha Gothard

"What does that mean?" Izzy asked out loud and glanced into the dark hall. She knew the moon would be full that very night. She was sure that's when Miss Bertie meant for her to come back to the theater, but the rest made no sense.

"Isabel, where are you?" Beth's words echoed in the alley.

Izzy grabbed the flowers and stuffed the note in her pocket.

"Be right there," she hollered and ran to meet Beth before her sister saw where Izzy had been.

Beth frowned at her from the alley entrance. Her hands rested on her hips. "Are you hiding to get out of all the work?"

Izzy walked toward Beth and said, "I needed to get these flowers for Grandma. And don't call me Isabel!"

Beth smirked and touched the lacy blooms with her fingertips. "Hey, they're kind of pretty," she said. Then she walked ahead of Izzy. "Come on. We need to do the dishes and then start loading the car."

"Be right there," Izzy called. When she came out of the alley, Izzy walked into the street and saw Miss Bertie in the center window above the theater's front doors. White hair framed her face.

Izzy whispered, "Tonight? When the moon is full?" Miss Bertie nodded and lowered the shade.

She'd thought about this night for what seemed like forever.

Longed to talk to Miss Bertie again.

Even made a list of what she wanted to say.

But now, all she wanted was a Founder's Day picnic and some fun. She wanted to forget why her dad wasn't laughing with Grandpa and about this moon stuff and Bertie Gothard. Izzy shivered in the blazing sun.

No way was she going into this dark alley at midnight.

CHAPTER 40

I zzy rubbed her stomach and groaned, "Oh, I ate too much."

"Good," Michael said, "That means more for me." He speared a hot dog with his fork.

"We still have Beth's cake and all that ice cream to eat," Grandma said.

Mom stood and stepped away from the picnic table. "Gotta walk off some potato salad before I can think about dessert."

Grandpa put his arms around Izzy and Beth and said, "Why don't you girls go for a little walk. I'll keep watch on everything while Michael inhales the rest of the hot dogs."

"I'd say you'll be taking a nap instead of guarding," Grandma said.

Grandpa laid back on a blanket under the tree. "Well now, since you suggested it, I think that is a fine idea." He tipped his hat over his eyes.

"Let's go, Grandma," Izzy said, "before Grandpa starts snoring."

Grandma laughed. Izzy hooked her arm and pulled her to the craft booths that looked like a village of tents along the bike path.

"I want to see everything!" Izzy twirled and pushed away the guilt that was constantly poking at her.

Happy felt good.

"Beth. Hey, Beth." Beth's friend, Kate, ran toward them. "Did you ask your mom?" Kate asked.

Izzy looked down at her feet and made designs in the dust with the toe of her flip-flop. She struggled to hang on to happy.

"Not yet," Beth said.

"Ask me what?" Mom crossed her arms.

"Kate wants me to go to the carnival then spend the night." Beth looked down. "I told her I wasn't sure since Grandma and Grandpa are here."

Izzy touched Miss Bertie's note in her pocket. Sneaking past an empty bed would be easier.

Except.

She wasn't going into that spooky building in the dark.

No way.

"Now, Vicki, I don't want to answer for you, but don't keep her home just because of us. We're staying a few days." Grandma smiled at Beth and winked.

Mom said, "Okay, Beth and Kate, why don't you go scout out the boy population or whatever else you have planned and meet us in about an hour for ice cream. You can go with Kate after that."

Mom must have been right on target about the boys because Beth's cheeks glowed.

"See you in an hour," Beth said. She reached over and gave Grandma a kiss. "Thanks." Then they were gone.

"Izzy," Mom said, "you lead the way."

For the next hour, they smelled lavender soap, touched a billion quilts, and sampled glazed cinnamon pecans. By the time Grandma bought Izzy a woven bracelet, and they picked one out for Beth, it was time to head back to wake up Grandpa.

****

"Izzy, you pass out the bowls and spoons," Grandma said. "Beth, you cut your cake. Michael, you can impress these girls with your muscles when you lift the ice cream freezer out of the trunk."

Beth and Izzy rolled their eyes.

"Izzy? Izzy, I've been looking everywhere for you." Ariel came running across the grass. Izzy handed the bowls to Beth and sprinted to her friend.

"Ariel! You're back." The girls hugged and squealed. "You can't believe how boring it's been without you," Izzy said.

Of course, she didn't share details about Dirty Bertie or the full-moon invitation.

The one she didn't plan to accept.

CHAPTER 41

aggert Creek's city park was a magnet on the warm summer night. As the sun dropped below the edge of the earth, streetlights buzzed to life. Squeals mingled with music over loud speakers and the roar of engines giving power to the carnival rides.

Ariel and Izzy cheered for their classmate as he threw darts at balloons in one of the games.

"Whoo! Just one more, Joel!"

"Go, go, go!"

He rubbed his palms together and winked in their direction.

They both squealed.

"Did you see that?" Ariel asked. "He's really good, isn't he?"

"Yep, and cute too," Izzy said. She slapped her hand over her mouth. They laughed until Izzy had to go in search of a porta-potty. Ariel kept a running explanation of every detail of her Nebraska trip through the thin walls of the little blue building. That was fine with Izzy. She didn't dare talk much.

"I didn't want to go, but Nebraska was awesome. Did I tell you I learned to water ski?" Ariel asked.

"Yes, twice," Izzy said. She pushed back the door and ran to a nearby spigot to wash her hands. Ariel's unending description of awesome Nebraska continued as they worked the crowd.

Izzy almost gave away her secrets when she glanced into the bleachers near the gazebo. There sat Bertie Gothard, on the second level eating popcorn and cheering for the mayor's speech. Wild white hair, long-sleeved dress, broom clenched in her gloved hands.

"Ugh-ugh."

"What's wrong?" Ariel slapped her on the back. "You swallow a bug or something?"

Izzy ran toward the bleachers. She turned back and grabbed Ariel's arm. "Look! She's right there." When she turned to point at Miss Bertie, the spot was empty. Izzy searched through the crowd with Ariel following. "She was there. You saw her, didn't you?"

"Who?" Ariel looked around at all the people and held her palms up.

"Miss Bertie, you know. Dirty Bertie! She was sitting on the bench eating popcorn with her broom across her lap. Remember? You heard her broom thumping in the theater." Izzy swallowed and whispered, "She had her broom with her, Ariel."

"Yeah, right. And I bet she was sitting by the pirate with toe fungus." Ariel laughed so hard people stared. "I can't believe you're still thinking about that. You are just too funny."

"Oh…yeah…funny, huh?" Izzy's heart pounded—she could barely speak—couldn't even say the pirate's name was Captain Crowbar.

Ariel grabbed her arm. "Come on. Let's ride the Ferris wheel so we can see the whole park."

Izzy followed Ariel.

She tried to breathe.

She tried to ignore the pictures that flashed in her head like exploding firecrackers. The fire, Cleopatra, Dad yelling at her, the dark alley, Miss Bertie's burning house, all of it rolled over and over in her mind.

She followed Ariel to the ticket booth to use some of the money Grandpa gave her. Squeezing her fists tight, she focused on the pain of her fingernails pressing into her palms. Hoped it would distract the other thoughts.

"You okay, Izzy?" Ariel asked as they waited in line. "I thought you liked the Ferris wheel."

"I do!" Izzy forced a smile. "Just excited, I guess."

Izzy wouldn't let herself think of anything but the lights, the shouts of the crowd, and the smell of diesel fuel as their rocking bench rose. Once all the seats were filled, the motor popped several times, and the big wheel rolled them over the top and down with a stomach fluttering loop.

Izzy squealed with Ariel every time they rode over the top. She could see the whole park but forced herself not to look toward the feed store and the theater. Way too soon, the operator began unloading passengers. Their pod stopped on top.

"Oh, look!" Ariel said. She pointed toward the ballpark on the south side of town. Someone was shooting off fireworks. There were bursts of red, orange, and green. The muffled pops floated across the trees.

Just as their seat began to inch over the top of the wheel, something else caught Izzy's eye in the distance. She gave a little gasp.

A huge round ball with a golden glow shone over the horizon.

A full.

Amber.

Moon.

CHAPTER 42

I
zzy felt squeezed in the silence of the feed store's office after the sounds of the carnival. Grandpa scraped the bottom of his ice cream bowl and sighed.

"You're awful quiet, Kiddo," he said. "Too much excitement today?"

Izzy set her plate on the sofa arm. "I guess."

The hum of the pop machine seemed amplified as Izzy considered telling Grandpa everything that was churning in her head. Even took a breath to begin when she heard her mom's and grandma's voices coming from the back of the store. Izzy stood and took Grandpa's empty bowl from his hand. Before she could get through the swinging door, she met Mom and Grandma coming from the back. Mom was laughing about something Grandma had said, and the sound made Izzy smile.

Grandma grabbed Izzy in a hug and asked, "Why don't you come stay with us at the motel tonight? You could swim in the pool."

Beth was spending the night at Kate's house, and Michael had gone home with Luke. Izzy had gotten strange looks when she turned down an invitation from Ariel. Grandma's offer was tempting. She could practically smell the chlorine from the pool.

"*Hm-hm-hm-hmmmm, hm-hmmm.*" Miss Bertie's melody filled Izzy's head before she could answer. She immediately was lost in the haunting notes.

"Isabel? Did you hear me?"

"Uh, I can't," Izzy said as the notes faded.

"Of course you can," Mom said. "Don't stay home because of me. I'll be fine."

"I'm so tired." Izzy faked a yawn. "I will tomorrow night. I want to sleep in my own bed tonight." The truth was, there wouldn't be much sleep, and her own bed still felt foreign. She knew, after seeing the amber moon, and no matter how much the thought of it scared her, she had an appointment with Miss Bertie.

"OK, sweetie. We understand." Izzy could tell her grandma's feelings were hurt, and she was tempted to tell them the truth.

Of course, she couldn't.

Grandpa stood and jingled the keys in his pocket. "We'd better go then so you girls can get some rest."

"Thanks to you both," Mom said. "Thanks for a great day. We'll see you in the morning."

"Bye. Love you." Izzy said and waved as her grandparents drove away. She wanted to run after them—to forget about the creepy theater and swim in the motel pool until she was exhausted. Then she'd sleep in a real room instead of beside storage boxes and crickets.

"No!" she whispered through her teeth.

"No, what?" Mom asked.

"Uh…there's…uh…no way I would have missed today. It was really fun." Izzy forced a smile.

"Me too," she said. "Well, it looks like it's just you and me tonight."

She and Mom walked arm and arm through the office door and were greeted by Maverick, who was still shaking from all the noises of the celebration. Izzy wrapped him in a hug.

Mom said, "You take Maverick for a quick walk while I see what kinds of messes need to be cleaned in the kitchen. I can't believe after all that food that I could eat another bite, but a piece of cake sounds pretty good."

"I'll take Maverick out, but I'm not hungry," Izzy said. "I'm so tired." She stretched. "I want to go right to bed." Izzy stared through the office windows. Light from the moon lit up the deserted park almost like daytime. *When the moon is full with amber light.*

Mom said, "Sure. It's been a big day." She gave Izzy a kiss on the top of her head.

It felt nice, safe.

"Mom?"

"What, sweetie?"

"Have you ever thought you heard…?"

"Heard what?" Mom's forehead wrinkled.

"Oh, nothing. Love you," Izzy said.

"I love you too. Everything's going to be fine. It's getting better every day." She patted Izzy on the arm, then checked the blinds. "Don't forget to lock the door."

Izzy clipped Maverick's leash to his collar and whispered in his ear, "Let's make this quick."

CHAPTER 43

Izzy woke with a jerk, disoriented in the dark, confused why she was still wearing the clothes she wore to the Founder's Day carnival. Something woke her. The wind? A gust rattled the roof and then another sound. She sat straight up—her eyes wide.

Ooooo..Isa...bel.

"Beth?" she whispered. No answer, then she remembered Beth was at Kate's.

Another rattle from the roof, *Isssaaabel...Isssaaabel.*

Izzy's whole body pulsed with the pounding of her heart, like a hammer slamming against her ribs.

It was time.

She slid from her bed, the concrete cool under her feet. She carried her flip-flops then tiptoed past Mom's room. In the kitchen, light leaked under the swinging door from the pop machine in the office. She inched the door forward and hurried to Maverick. He whined and licked her cheek.

"Did you hear that noise?" His tail thumped on the floor. Izzy ran her hand along his side. She looked into his eyes and felt his breath going in and out. She sat with his head in her lap until her heart stopped racing.

The wind picked up and rattled the front door. *Issaabell. Issaabell.*

"Did you hear that, Maverick?" She hugged him tight, but he just sighed and closed his eyes. "That noise. It sounded like my name.

When the moon is full with amber light,

And the wind is whispering your name,

Truth revealed with second sight,

No one left to blame.

"This is crazy, but I have to go," she said to the dog. "The wind. It...it called my name." She went to Mom's desk to get the office key. She reached for the doorknob but turned back when she heard Maverick unwinding from his spot.

"No, boy. I have to go alone. I'll be back though—I hope."

She eased the door open, then pressed it shut behind her and turned the key in the lock. The moon was high in the sky, peeking in and out from shadowing clouds. Izzy tuned in to every sound—the hum of the streetlights, the barking of a dog.

The beating of her heart.

Back pressed against the outside walls of the office, the scent of the sleeping carnival and damp earth made her nose itch. She walked sideways, fingers sliding along the concrete blocks of the office building, still warm from the sun. At the edge, she stretched to reach the feed building corner, afraid to let go. She grabbed the side of the building and pulled herself toward it. Inch by inch until she came to that building's edge. Then she peeked into the alley. It stretched back, back, back—so much further in the dark.

"This is stupid. I'm going back."

An engine roared down the street. Izzy slid around the corner and into the shadows of the alley. Pressing her body against the brick wall, she held her breath while two cars with booming speakers raced past then squealed around the corner onto Main Street. She'd heard the same kids racing through town late on Saturday nights—trying to outrun the town's lone police car. Her mind jumped back to that same policeman handing mom a steaming cup the night of the fire. She shivered.

The tires squealed in the distance, and she thought of a million reasons why she should run back to her bed. Her feet crunched on the gravel as she turned away from the long stretch of darkness. The wind picked up, blowing dust and bits of paper against her legs. It whistled between the two buildings, and the sound grew louder.

Issaabell. Issaabell.

Izzy slid her fingers into her pocket. Miss Bertie's note crinkled under her touch. She whispered the words, "When the moon is full, with amber light, and the wind is whispering your name...whispering your name."

"Meow." Cleopatra sat on the old car's hood at the other end of the alley. Her green eyes glowed. They were magnets pulling Izzy away from her safe spot. Once she let go of the wall, she ran into the darkness and slid to a stop in front of the cat's throne.

"Hello to you too," Izzy whispered.

"Hello, Isabel."

Izzy skidded to the other side of the car to escape whoever had spoken her name.

Tap, tap, tap.

She dropped to her knees and covered her head with her hands. "Dear God, help me," she whispered.

Cold fingers clamped on her shoulder.

CHAPTER 44

"Isabel, dear. Why are you hiding?"

Izzy recognized Miss Bertie's voice and felt such unbelievable relief.

Until she looked up.

"Awgh!" She scooted backward on her bottom against the car. "Who are you?" She jumped to her feet, fingers gliding along the sides of the car, stopping when she felt the broken taillights. She turned her body and slipped to the other side of the car. She felt safer somehow, with the car between her and whoever this hideous person was.

"It's me, Isabel." The figure took a step toward her. Tap...tap... tap. Just then, the full moon slipped from a bank of clouds and filled the end of the alley with moonlight. Cleopatra jumped from the hood of the car and into the person's arms.

"There you are, Cleopatra. I'm afraid we have given Isabel a fright." The lady smiled, and Izzy caught sight of her eyes in the moonlight.

"Miss Bertie?" Izzy took a few steps toward her. "It is you, isn't it?"

The woman laughed, "Well, of course. Who else would it be?" She raised her hand to her cheek. "Oh, of course. I forgot about my costume." She raised her gloved hand to her head and down past her clothes to her feet. "Do you like it?"

Izzy inched around the back of the car to get a closer look. Miss Bertie's hair was dark and was rolled around her head in the back. Her dress was heavy material with thick shoulder pads. None of that was so scary, but her face made Izzy's skin crawl. The old woman's skin glowed in the moonlight like chalky cream, and her lips were blue outlined in black.

"You'll understand soon, dear." Miss Bertie indicated the open door to the back of the theater. "Shall we go in? We don't want to be late." She turned with a swish of her skirts and tap scooted across the gravel-littered pavement to the open door. Cleopatra started to follow her then stopped to meow at Izzy.

"Okay," Izzy said, "I'll go, but I can't stay long." She followed into the dark hallway. They didn't seem to need any light, but Izzy stooped to pick up the flashlight from the wooden box. The beam caught the constant dust dancing in the air. Goosebumps popped up on her arms when the temperature dropped like they'd walked into winter. She was halfway down the hall when the thumping of the broom stopped.

"Miss Bertie?" Izzy turned the light in different directions, catching glimpses of the dinosaur-shaped stain on the ceiling and Captain Crowbar's pirate sneer. Her heart hammered.

"Miss Bertie? Please, wait for me." Izzy heard the terror in her own voice. She walked a little faster past the strangely silent Captain Crowbar and toward the familiar stairs and red door. A wind gust from outside rattled the plywood-covered windows beside her, and she started to run.

"*Issaabel. Issaabel.*" The sound surrounded her.

"Miss Bertie? Help!" Izzy screamed.

"Thump, thump, thump," sounded behind her. She slowed and turned to walk toward the sound.

"Aaaaagggghhh!" Izzy screamed. Miss Bertie's face glowed in the flashlight beam. The shadows made her face even more spooky.

"Isabel, dear? There is no reason to be so frightened. Follow me."

Miss Bertie disappeared through a door in the wall Izzy had never noticed. The echo of the broom against the floor sounded like she was leading her into a huge room. Izzy walked through the doorway. Icy air blew into her face causing her teeth to chatter. She stopped when the flashlight went dark.

"Miss Bertie? I'm afraid."

Izzy startled when Miss Bertie's bony hand touched her back, guiding her, pressing her forward. A soft glow, almost like moon-light, pooled around them.

"We must hurry, dear. The performance will soon begin. Ahhh...see, here are our seats."

"But, I don't understand." Izzy's heart pounded even harder, her throat so dry the words scratched.

"Patience, dear." She dropped into one of the faded velvet-cov-ered seats with a grunt and motioned for Izzy to join her. Dusty sheets covered row after row of seats across the slanted floor. When Izzy hesitated, Miss Bertie pulled her into the seat.

Izzy's courage was fading. "I want to go home. Please, can I go home now? Mom will be looking for me."

"Of course, you may go home—any time you want. But you may want to wait until after the performance." Miss Bertie smiled a strange eerie grin. "That's why you came, isn't it?

191

"No," Izzy said, although it had to be true. "You said to come when the moon was full, so that's what I did. And what performance?"

Miss Bertie's hand rested on Izzy's, and the old woman leaned closer. Her foul breath puffed into Izzy's face with each word of the poem she quoted.

"When the moon is full with amber light,

And the wind is whispering your name,

Truth revealed with second sight,

No one left to blame."

The dim light refocused on the stage. A whisper of mustiness tickled Izzy's nose when the tattered stage curtains glided open. "I really need to leave." She stood, but her legs buckled like they were made of rubber. She fell into the seat.

Miss Bertie leaned back in her chair. "We must stop conversing now, Isabel. *The Performance of the Dead* is beginning."

CHAPTER 45

T he stage was set with a blackboard, wooden benches, and tables. Two girls in old-fashioned dresses and laced-up black boots walked into the light and turned to face Miss Bertie and Izzy. They looked a little younger than Izzy and her sister. Their faces had the same pasty white glow and dark lips that Miss Bertie's did.

"Hi, Izzy," the younger one said, then she waved and giggled.

"Stop, Hattie. You're ruining the play," said the older girl.

Izzy turned to Miss Bertie and squeaked, "I've heard that giggle before, in the theater that first day. Do those girls live here too?"

Miss Bertie patted Izzy's hand. She shivered at the coldness of the woman's touch through her gloves.

The older girl smoothed her dress and said, "Welcome to our play. My name is Elizabeth." She curtsied then motioned toward the other girl. "This is my sister, Hattie." The little girl curtsied also, then giggled behind her hand.

"It was April 4, 1883, at our little schoolhouse just outside Taggert Creek," Elizabeth said.

Hattie stepped forward. "Miss Whitaker asked me to recite the poem I was learning for our community program." Hattie stood by the chalkboard, and Elizabeth sat on one of the benches.

Hattie folded her hands in front of her and said, "*A Psalm of Life* by Henry Wadsworth Longfellow." She cleared her throat and began.

"Tell me not, in mournful numbers,

Life is but an empty dream! —

For the soul is dead that slumbers,

And things are not what they seem."

Hattie looked down, then turned to her sister and said, "That's all I remember, but it's a very long poem."

"I know, Hattie. They understand," Elizabeth shaded her eyes with her hand and said, "Don't you, Miss Bertie?"

Izzy jumped when Miss Bertie spoke, "We certainly do, don't we, Isabel?"

Izzy's voice wouldn't work, so she just nodded. She had to be stumbling through a nightmare and wanted so much to make it stop. She gripped the arms of her chair till her knuckles were white.

"Please continue, girls," Miss Bertie said.

Elizabeth said to her sister, "Tell what happened, Hattie."

"Well, just as I finished saying my poem, and Miss Whitaker told me I could sit down, two of the older boys in the back started arguing." She rolled her eyes. "You know, boys."

Miss Bertie cleared her throat.

"Oh, well, anyway, they started shoving one another, and they knocked over the wood stove."

Izzy sat forward in her seat when she smelled smoke and saw flames that filled the stage. Miss Bertie put her hand on Izzy's arm and said, "Not to worry, Isabel dear, just theatrics."

Izzy wasn't quite sure what theatrics meant, but Miss Bertie wasn't worried, so she tried to relax. Elizabeth's scream and words took away any relaxed feeling.

"Hurry, Hattie, take my hand."

"I can't go yet, Elizabeth. I left the locket Papa gave me by my slate." Hattie pulled her arm free of Elizabeth's grasp.

"No, Hattie, don't go back into the smoke." Elizabeth went after her sister, and the stage went black.

The only sound Izzy could hear was the wind whistling through the roof. "Miss Bertie, she whispered in the dark, "did they get out of the fire?" She wanted to cover her ears to block the answer.

"No, dear, they did not," Miss Bertie said. "But there is more."

****

The silvery spotlight shone again in the center of the stage. The scent of roses overshadowed the smoke. On the stage stood a woman all in white. She carried a bouquet of roses, and the man standing with her was wearing a uniform.

"Oh, a wedding," Izzy said and turned to Miss Bertie with a hopeful look.

Miss Bertie shook her head slowly back and forth and said, "Watch the play, Isabel."

Booming organ music filled the theater. The dark-sounding notes were familiar to Izzy, just like Hattie's giggle.

A voice said, "I now pronounce you husband and wife. You may kiss your bride." The couple gave each other a shy kiss then turned to face the audience.

Izzy gasped when the spotlight shone on their chalky faces and blue-tinged lips. They smiled and stepped to the edge of the stage.

"We were so happy, weren't we, Frank?" The woman smiled.

"That we were, Mary." He raised her hand to gently kiss it. "But, our time was short." He smiled at his bride. "The date was March 7, 1916, in Taggert Creek."

"Our first day as husband and wife," Mary said, "and we only had one night before Frank was to ship out to the war in France. We wanted the day to be perfect." They stepped out of the light, and the scene changed to a small kitchen. Mary was wearing an apron around her waist and carried plates to a cloth-covered table. The backdoor opened, and Frank said, "This ought to be enough for tonight. Sure was nice of your brother to cut wood for us."

"It was nice, wasn't it?" Mary said. She carried a steaming bowl to the table.

"I'll build it up before we go to sleep, and it should still be warm in the morning when you fix my breakfast." He scratched his head. "I should have thought to get a screen for the front. I'll get one at the hardware store before my train leaves." He took Mary in his arms. "I'd hate the thought of you here alone with an open fire." Frank and Mary sat at the table to eat their wedding supper.

The stage went dark except for the blazing fire in the fireplace. A large log slipped from the fire and rolled onto the rug in front of it. A pale light shone on the bedroom where Frank and Mary were asleep. Smoke slipped under the door. Mary raised up.

"Frank, I smell smoke."

Darkness.

"Miss Bertie, I don't like these plays," Izzy said. She pulled her knees to her chest and wrapped her arms over her head. "Why are you making me watch this?"

Miss Bertie's cold hand reached for Izzy's. "I think you know, Isabel. There are only two scenes left, and you must see them."

Izzy dropped her feet to the floor and turned toward Miss Bertie. "But why? Why do I need to see people die in fires?" Izzy shook her head back and forth. "I don't want to think about any of this." She tried to stand again, but this time Miss Bertie stood with her.

"You may leave at any time, Isabel dear. But if you want the answers you have been seeking, you must watch." Miss Bertie smiled. "Shhh, the next scene is beginning."

****

An older man and woman sat around a table with a young soldier. Their faces were the same pasty white with dark lips. A side door opened, and another woman carried a round cake with white frosting.

Izzy strained to see the face of the woman who spoke. "That lady looks just like…" She turned to Miss Bertie, but the seat beside her was empty. Glancing around the dim theater then back to the stage, Izzy whispered, "Miss Bertie?"

From the table where she set the cake, a slow nod of the woman's head told Izzy that Miss Bertie was a member of the cast in this play. An uneasiness stirred in Izzy's stomach.

Miss Bertie turned to face the audience of one. "It was December 24, 1944," she said. Izzy squirmed in her seat, recognizing the date. "My parents, Abner, and Esther Gothard, and my fiancé, Tom, and I were celebrating Christmas Eve."

BERTIE AND TOM 1943

Izzy remembered the brick in the alley that her fingers had slid over so many times.

"Meow."

On the stage, Miss Bertie bent to pick up Cleopatra. "Oh yes, I almost forgot you. Cleopatra was celebrating with us also. Scat now." The cat jumped from her arms. "You've already had your supper."

Izzy smiled, remembering all the times Cleopatra had led Maverick in a chase. "What? That's not possible," she whispered. If Cleopatra had been there, that would make the cat really old. Cats didn't live that long.

The older lady began cutting huge slices of the cake and said, "Tom, just wait until you taste Bertie's special Christmas cake. The recipe has been in our family since the Civil War." She handed a plate with cake on it to Tom. "Bertie has been saving ration stamps for months to get enough sugar."

The scent of cinnamon and raisins floated across the stage. Izzy remembered the cake Miss Bertie made for her birthday.

The older gentleman took a drink from his cup. Izzy wondered if it was Earl Grey tea. "That's my little girl. She's a good manager, Tom," he said, "and she'll make you a fine wife."

The scene changed to a different room with a fireplace and comfy chairs. A huge Christmas tree stood by the curve of the stairs.

"Oh, it's beautiful, just beautiful." Miss Bertie's mother hugged her.

"Wait, Mother. You haven't seen the best part," Miss Bertie said.

Tom crawled on the floor behind the tree, and suddenly the whole tree was lit with big colored lights.

"Well, look at that," Miss Bertie's father said. "I thought the bulbs all burned out last year. Where in the world did you find new ones?"

"At a hardware store in Atchison." Miss Bertie's dark lips stretched into a smile.

"Well, they're just beautiful." The lights blinked and then went out.

Miss Bertie reached for Tom's arm. "It must have come loose from the outlet." Tom crawled under the tree, and the lights came on bright again.

"I'd say we can enjoy them for a bit then unplug." He crawled from the tree and stood with his arm around Miss Bertie. "The bulbs are new, but that cord is frayed near the plug. I'll fix it in the morning."

Miss Bertie's father walked to the window and pulled back the drapes. "Plan on staying here tonight, Tom. There's ice over everything," said Mr. Gothard.

"Why don't you head on to bed," said Mrs. Gothard. "The guest room is ready, and I see you can hardly hold your eyes open."

"Thanks." He rubbed the back of his neck. "I didn't sleep much coming back from boot camp on the train." He turned and kissed Miss Bertie on the cheek, then climbed the stairs.

"Momma and Poppa, why don't you both go on to bed too. I have a bit left on the scarf I'm knitting Tom."

"Of course. Don't stay up too late, Bertie dear," said Mrs. Gothard. "You will remember to unplug the lights on the tree?"

"Yes, Mother, I just want to enjoy them a little longer."

Miss Bertie's parents walked up the stairs, and she was alone. She walked to a wooden radio on a small table and twisted one of the dials on the side.

Izzy expected to hear Christmas music. What she heard took her breath.

What'll I do, when you are far away, and I'm so blue? What'll I do?...

It was the song that had haunted Izzy's thoughts since the first time she heard Miss Bertie hum it. The same song Mrs. Bartlett said Miss Bertie wouldn't quit humming after her house burned.

On the stage, Miss Bertie picked up a bag from beside the sofa and pulled out a long scarf and some yarn. Long knitting needles clicked in her fingers with each stitch and kept time with her humming. Cleopatra jumped into her lap. Soon Miss Bertie's head drooped, and she was asleep.

"Pop! Flash!"

There was a spark, and in seconds, flames ate up the branches of the tree. Smoke blocked out the scene, and the air vibrated with a scream like Izzy had never heard before.

Izzy curled into a ball, covering her ears with her hands, rocking back and forth until everything in the theater went dark and silent. She stood and shouted into the blackness, "Miss Bertie? Miss Bertie! Where are you?"

CHAPTER 46

A cold hand touched Izzy's shoulder. "What happened in the fire, Miss Bertie? You got out, didn't you, before...?"

"You know the answer, dear. Remember, you talked to my dear friend, Mrs. Bartlett? You'll understand the rest soon."

Izzy dropped into her seat. How did the woman know she'd been to Mrs. Bartlett's house and what they talked about? And, if they were such dear friends, why didn't Mrs. Bartlett know Miss Bertie was still alive—or was she? Izzy reluctantly turned to look at the woman beside her. Miss Bertie no longer wore the gloves. The skin on her fingers and arms was tight with hideous scars. Bile burned Izzy's throat, and she stood.

"I don't want to see any more. I'm going home." Izzy searched for the door.

"There's just one more play." Miss Bertie's shoulders heaved with a huge sigh. "And this...well, this is the most important one of all. But, Isabel, like I've told you before, the choice to stay or not is yours."

A light appeared in the center of the stage in what looked like Izzy's room in the trailer before it burned. Izzy swallowed hard then gasped for air.

"No, no!" she shouted. "I can't watch this." She shook her head and backed away.

"It is the only way, dear." Miss Bertie said softly, then all was quiet. She didn't pull Izzy back, didn't force her to sit and relive that horrible night. Yet, Izzy returned to her seat and stared at the scene in front of her.

She saw herself on the top bunk, but it wasn't really her. It was Hattie from the first play. She was reading Izzy's book with a flashlight. Her white face, so disturbing in the shadows of the light she held. On the bottom bunk was another girl dressed like Beth but played by Hattie's sister.

Then a second light shone on the kitchen table. There was a man with his head resting against his arms. A square bottle sat nearby, and his fingers gripped a glass. Izzy wondered if Miss Bertie's Tom was playing this part. None of it made sense. Tom died in the fire. They'd all died in fires. That would make them all...

There was a groan from the man at the table, and he raised his head as if it were heavy. When Izzy saw the pasty white face with blue-tinged lips, she thought her heart was going to explode.

It was her father.

Izzy shook her head to clear the crazy thoughts. "It can't be him," she said. "He's...dead." Her eyes met Miss Bertie's. The old woman looked so sad. "How can it be him?" Izzy whispered. She turned back to the stage. "Daddy?" she said a little louder. She wanted to run to him, to tell him she didn't mean to start the fire. But, he was dead. Like all the others.

On the stage, Dad stood and stumbled away from the table, falling onto his stomach on the couch. The stage went dark. A spotlight showed Izzy's character sliding from her bed and creeping to the bathroom. A match was lit, and the girl's chalky face glowed in the light from the candle. The sweet vanilla smell made Izzy cringe. She pulled her knees to her chest and wrapped her arms around them. "No, no, no. Please don't make me watch this. I know what happened."

Miss Bertie's cold hand reached for Izzy's. "I can't force you to watch. But, everything isn't as it seems. Please look up, Isabel."

Izzy looked, then held her breath. She jumped when Dad pulled open the door and yelled to get to bed. She waited for the book to close and...

There was a puff of air from the girl's lips as she leaned over the candle. The scene went dark when the flame was gone.

"That's not what happened." Izzy's throat ached with tightness. "I forgot to blow it out, and then the trailer burned, and Dad, he died." Her head began to swim. "It was my fault!" The guilt she'd pushed down and bottled up for months came gushing from her lips. "I killed my dad!"

The words echoed through the empty seats, bounced off the walls, traveled away from her, never to be taken back. She ran to slam her fists on the stage's edge. "I'm sorry! I wanted to read. But, I didn't mean for you to die!"

Miss Bertie stood and leaned close. "Of course, you didn't mean for him to die, but you're wrong about the events." Her breath was near Izzy's ear. "There's more to this story." Izzy dropped back into the seat, shaking, praying for all of it to be over. She raised her head and stared at the stage.

The light shone on the bathroom scene. It was no longer Izzy in the room but her dad. The sound of his body throwing up the alcohol was sickening. Dad stood, then dropped to the side of the tub dragging the back of his hand across his mouth.

Izzy bit her lip until she tasted blood. She waited for her father to leave the bathroom, but he didn't. He pulled a cigarette from the pack he kept in his front pocket, then struck a match. The end of the cigarette glowed, and the smell of burning tobacco floated across the stage. The glow grew brighter when he pulled in smoke then blew it out to float above his head. Dad grunted when he stood, tried to take a step forward, and fell against the sink. He grabbed the cigarette dangling from his lips and flung it across the bathroom. It fell in the trashcan, where the glow grew brighter. He stumbled through the doorway and collapsed in the hall. A flame jumped above the rim of the trashcan.

"Beep-beep-beep." Izzy squeezed her eyes shut as the sounds of the fire echoed through the theater.

And then, silence.

"Isabel. Open your eyes." Miss Bertie's voice sounded far away.

"I can't. Why are you making me watch it?" Izzy curled into a tight ball and turned in the seat away from the scene. "Please don't make me watch," she moaned and rocked back and forth.

"No more fires, dear. Just open your eyes."

Izzy peeked through eye slits. The stage was dark, and the dusty curtains were closed. She sat in a pool of filmy light. "Miss Bertie?" she said. But the seat beside her was empty. "Miss Bertie?" Izzy stood and turned in all directions. A sense of downing made her gasp for air. "Where are you?"

She had to get out.

The glow of light around her was swallowed into darkness a few steps beyond where she stood. The flashlight! She'd picked it up when she came in the back door. Her foot hit something and rolled toward the stage.

That's when she saw the note.

All sound was gone except Izzy's breath. The paper crackled when she unfolded it.

When the moon was full with amber light,
And the wind was whispering your name,
You learned the truth with second sight,
No one left to blame.
Decisions were made, wrong or right.
Our guilt was all the same.
The past, impossible to rewrite,
Your choice—let go of the pain.

Izzy looked up and saw light glint off something else on the stage's edge. She reached for it. A familiar smoothness cooled her palm. Mind racing, she remembered the shape, the painted face, Dad's smile when he gave it to her. She held the little china dog against her lips. But, it couldn't be the same one. It was gone, burned up in the fire just like everything else.

"Miss Bertie, where are you? Help me understand." A breeze from nowhere caught the note Izzy had dropped and blew it against her leg. She picked it up, her eyes catching the final line again. "Your choice...let go of the pain."

Izzy squeezed the china dog in her fist and slumped into a seat with her arms covering her head. A moan came from so deep inside, Izzy thought she was going to pass out. All the guilt she'd kept a secret for so long exploded like a break in a dam.

She cried.

She screamed.

She tried to let it go.

CHAPTER 47

Beth pulled the pillow from her sister's head. "Better hurry. Grandma and Grandpa are picking us up for church, then we're going out to eat."

Izzy rolled over and mumbled under her pillow, "Too tired." She sat up and rubbed her eyes. "I thought you were at Kate's."

"I was, but they dropped me off early before they left for a family thing in Topeka. Mom's not going to be happy you slept in your clothes."

Izzy looked down and remembered—the plays, the poem. Then leaving the theater with legs so rubbery, she couldn't take another step. She dropped under Miss Bertie's brick, where she tried to make sense of what she'd seen.

Four plays, all with fires, everyone died. She saw her dad, her *dead* dad. They were all dead. But what about Miss Bertie? No, she couldn't be dead. She'd made Izzy tea and cookies. She'd come into their store and wrote notes and poems. Mrs. Bartlett said those were just stories about Dirty Bertie haunting the theater—didn't she?

The last thing Izzy remembered from the alley was Cleopatra purring and rubbing against her legs while she sat under the carved brick. She didn't know how long she sat there in the dark or how she got back to the store. Izzy shook her head. Maybe none of it happened. She looked down at her hand. It hurt to uncurl her fingers where the china dog was wedged tight in her fist. "If it wasn't real, how did I get this?"

"What did you say?" asked Beth.

"Uh...how come we're going to church?"

"Grandma called Mom early this morning and said she wants us to all go together—especially since the church helped us so much after the fire. Mom agreed with her." Beth stood in front of the small wall mirror, brushing her hair. "Get ready. We're leaving in thirty minutes. Picking up Michael on the way."

Izzy slid from the top bunk and stretched. She glanced around the plywood box room. If Dad hadn't been drinking that night. If he hadn't lit the cigarette. The "ifs" made her head hurt. She slipped the ceramic dog in the pocket of the dress she would wear to church and went to the kitchen. Mom was making toast.

"Hurry up and eat a bite before you shower," she said, then looked at Izzy over her glasses. "Did you sleep in your clothes last night?"

Izzy shrugged her shoulders and wolfed down a whole piece of toast and half her milk. "Mom?" she said, "I need to talk to you." She spooned grape jam onto a second piece of toast.

"Okay, but make it quick." Mom unplugged the toaster and wiped crumbs from the cabinet.

"I know how the fire started."

Mom stopped cleaning and sat across from her. "What do you mean?"

"Dad threw a cigarette in the trash, didn't he?" Mom looked at her hands.

"Yes, the fire department thinks it started in the bathroom trash can. I've wondered if it wasn't a cigarette. How did you know?" Mom's forehead was scrunched.

"I heard someone talking." That wasn't exactly true, but Izzy wasn't about to tell her she'd seen her dead father in a play last night. "Why didn't you tell us?"

"I'm sorry. I didn't think it was something you needed to know. It wouldn't help to bring him back if I told you." Tears pooled in her eyes.

"I know. I just feel better knowing how it happened." Izzy scooted toast crumbs with her finger into a line on the table.

"Are you mad at him, Mom?" She didn't mean to ask that.

Mom was quiet and picked at her fingers. Suddenly she looked up and said, "Yes, I'm so mad at him I can't even describe it, but it doesn't change anything. I hope someday I can let it go." She stood. "Now, get in the shower. I don't want to tromp into church late with everyone watching."

****

Mom didn't want to be late, but songs were already being sung when they slipped into the back row of the church. It seemed like such a long time since they'd eaten ice cream, and Izzy rode the Ferris wheel. Grandma blew her nose, and Grandpa put his arm around her.

"Welcome, everyone," Pastor Smith said.

Izzy knew she was supposed to be serious, but all she could think of was the burping conversation she'd had with the minister when he visited them at the store. She covered her mouth to keep from giggling. Mom thumped her on the arm like she could hear Izzy's thoughts.

At the end of the service, Pastor Smith said, "We're glad to have the Dunn family with us this morning. We're praying for you as you grieve and forgive the past."

Why did he say, forgive? Did he know Dad started the fire?

Forgive.

Izzy pushed out the breath she was holding. She wished she could rewind the last six months, and everyone could have a do-over. She wished all the people in the plays could go back in their time and change what happened.

Forgive.

Izzy touched the china dog in her pocket. Then the service was over, and Beth was herding her out of the seat.

They went to the new restaurant out on the highway. While they were eating, Grandma wiped her mouth with a napkin and said, "Vicky, there's one more thing we need to do today."

Mom took a sip of iced tea. "What's that?"

Grandma's eyes flicked for a moment toward Grandpa. Then she cleared her throat. "We should go to the cemetery." She blew out her breath.

No one spoke.

Beth and Michael stopped eating and looked down at their laps.

Mom moved her salad around in the bowl.

As far as Izzy knew, no one had been back to the cemetery since the day of the funeral. The guilt she'd lived with so long pulsed into her thoughts. Her cheeseburger felt dry in her throat.

Michael cleared his throat. "Grandma's right. We need to go." It was strange to see him take charge. He pressed his lips together—just like Dad.

Mom looked out the window, raking her thumbnail across her lips. A twanging country song vibrated from speakers.

People laughed.

Silverware clinked against plates.

Ice plunked into glasses.

Mom turned. A little smile stretched her lips. "Yes, Michael, it's time.

CHAPTER 48

Grandpa drove the car around the twisting road past the stone markers. Izzy tried to read the stones that marked the graves. Then the car stopped, and everyone turned in the same direction. DUNN was carved in dark letters against a simple grey piece of rock. The dirt in front of the marker was still mounded with no grass growing on it. Izzy tried not to think of Dad being under the mound in his new shirt and tie.

"Vicky," Grandma sniffed and used a tissue to dab at her eyes, "it looks real nice."

"Sure does," Grandpa said. "I'll get the flowers from the trunk."

"Thank you," Mom said to Grandma, then she hugged her. "I was just wishing I had brought some." Grandpa's feet crunched in the dry grass. He handed mom a bouquet of artificial sunflowers. The happy flowers.

"Here you go, Vicky. You put them like you want."

Mom kneeled to drop some in each vase on the sides of the square rock. Anger bubbled up in Izzy. How could Dad let himself be so drunk he didn't think how one cigarette could change their lives. But then, Izzy remembered the play. She wished she had something to put there too—a way to thank Dad for coming back in the theater—for showing her what happened the night of the fire. Her hand went to the pocket of her skirt where she had put the china dog before they left for church. It felt smooth and cool in her fingers. She pulled it from her pocket and held it in the palm of her hand.

"What's that?" Beth asked.

"Oh, just something I found," Izzy said." She slipped it back in her pocket.

"I think we're ready now," Mom said.

As the car was leaving, it passed the oldest graves in the cemetery. Izzy saw a familiar name blur by.

"Grandpa? Stop the car." She unbuckled her seatbelt and turned in the seat.

"Are you sick?" he asked.

"No, I just want to see something."

Mom answered for him, "No, sweetie, it's too hot. Let's not stop now."

Izzy watched the dust swirl from the turning tires behind them and drew a mental map of where the name GOTHARD stood out on the tallest stone.

****

"Are you sure you don't want to spend the rest of the summer with us?" Grandma asked the morning they were going back to Missouri. "The neighbor has some new kittens that you would like." Izzy wondered if any of the kittens were grey with haunting green eyes. She was tempted, but she had unfinished business.

"I'd really like to," Izzy said, "but Ariel's back, and we don't have much time before school starts."

"Well, let us know if you change your mind. We could meet your mother halfway later." They crawled into their car and soon were heading for the highway.

Mom ran her fingers through her hair. "Time to get back to work."

Izzy turned when the weathervane squeaked on top of the theater. So much had changed since the day they moved into the back of the store. She wished she could tell Mom about Miss Bertie and the plays. Maybe someday.

Mom turned to walk into the office, but Izzy stopped her. "I think I'll go for a walk."

"Going to the library?" Mom grabbed the broom from inside the office and swept dried grass from the sidewalk in front of the store.

Izzy decided to be truthful for a change.

"I want to go to the cemetery to check on the sunflowers we left." Izzy pushed some of the dry grass into a little pile with the toe of her sandal. "And," she added, "I want to look for the stone I saw on Sunday." Mom stopped sweeping.

"Are you okay?" she asked.

"I'm fine," Izzy said. "I liked going to see Dad's, you know, his grave.

Mom smiled. "I'm glad it helped." She rested her chin on the broom handle.

It reminded Izzy of Miss Bertie. Was she watching from the top windows?

"I can go with you this evening after we close the store." Mom leaned down to look into Izzy's eyes.

"No, I'll be alright." Izzy reached her hands around the back of her head to pull her ponytail tighter.

Mom rubbed gentle circles on Izzy's back. Then she glanced at her watch. "Just be back by ten o'clock. I have some chores for you."

"Ten. Got it," Izzy said, walking backward. Then she turned and trotted along the uneven sidewalk. Sweat trickled down her back. She slowed her pace when she passed the trailer court. All that was left was a blank space—like their life there had never happened.

Izzy turned and focused on the cemetery in the distance. Its grey stones reminded her of little houses. The air sizzled with heat, and cicadas made clicking vibrations from nearby trees. Her feet kicked up dust as she walked toward the arch stretched across the cemetery's entrance.

Just inside the gate, Izzy scanned the stones on the third road until she saw the tallest one. Her heart began to pound. It was a huge marker made of rock that reminded her of the steps in the vacant lot where Miss Bertie's house once stood. Across the front of the marker, in large letters, GOTHARD was chiseled with some words.

Though I walk through the valley of the shadow of death, I will fear no evil.

23rd Psalm.

Izzy remembered the minister reading the same words on that cold day under the blue tent. She glanced across the cemetery to her dad's grave, then kneeled and ran her fingers over the carved words.

"ESTHER GOTHARD, June 2, 1900 – December 24, 1944." She moved to the stone beside it. "ABNER GOTHARD, October 20, 1899 – December 24, 1944." She wiped her eyes with the back of her hand and glanced to the left. There was another stone with a last name that seemed familiar.

"GRIFFIN," she read, then crawled to get a closer look. "Tom Griffin, May 30, 1920 – December 24, 1944." She moved her fingers across his name. "Oh, Miss Bertie. It's your Tom." Izzy remembered the picture Mrs. Bartlett showed her—the smiling Tom and young Miss Bertie.

She stood and stared into the distance. The song came to her, not intense like before, but more of a memory of something she'd heard. The notes faded into the buzz of insects and a motorcycle zooming by in a cloud of dust.

Izzy glanced to the right. Another stone. Strange, she hadn't noticed it before. She kneeled for a closer look. Her hand flew to her mouth

"Bertha (Bertie) Gothard."

Izzy looked toward the town—the tower of Miss Bertie's theater baked in heatwaves. Mrs. Bartlett said she didn't die in the fire.

"So," Izzy whispered, "why am I afraid to look?" She felt light-headed, and her body tingled. She forced herself to read the rest of the chiseled words on the stone.

"Born March 16, 1924 - Died July 4, 1990." Izzy fell on the grass like she'd gotten a jolt of electricity. She remembered Mrs. Bartlett's words. *Now, Isabel, I'm sure you've heard the rumors that she haunts that old theater.*

Izzy played back all the conversations with Miss Bertie. The tea and cookies, the performance in the theater. Cleopatra.

None of it made sense. Maybe she should tell Mrs. Bartlett. Maybe she could explain.

Izzy closed her eyes and pictured Miss Bertie, framed by the windows above the theater, her finger to her lips. No, the old woman trusted her with this secret. She couldn't tell.

Izzy wiped dried grass from the base of the stone and sat back on her knees. "Thank you, Miss Bertie. I don't understand but thank you for showing me the truth."

Izzy traced Bertie's name one more time, then stood and walked toward the mound of dirt near the edge of the fence. She wrapped her fingers around the china dog in her pocket—the paper she brought with her crinkled beside it.

Kneeling to the side of her dad's stone, she touched the artificial flowers Mom had put in the vases. The happy flowers. She moved from her knees to sit on the ground—the weight of what she had to do causing her breath to quicken.

Trembling, she pulled the paper from her pocket. Unfolded and smoothed it against her thigh. She pulled in grass-cooked air and blew it out.

"I don't know if you can hear me, but I have to...I need to read something out loud." Wind swooped in and moved the flowers.

#1 "Why were you so mad all the time?" Izzy waited, listening for an answer. But the only sound was the metal flag rigging clanking against the pole. The wind kicked up tiny pieces of grit, and a meadowlark chanted in the field.

Your fault.

Your fault.

Your fault.

"No! It wasn't my fault!" She shouted, and the bird swooped away.

She sucked in a deep breath and choked out the rest.

#2 "Why did you pull my hair? You used to rock me and hug me. And one of my last memories is going to be you pulling my hair."

#3. "Why did you say that horrible thing to Michael about never being anything more than he is now. That's just wrong! Mom should have told you to stop. I should have."

#4 "I'm mad at you for drinking and turning into someone I didn't like. And for throwing the cigarette." "I love you because you're my dad, but...I'm really mad at you." Saying the words felt wrong and right at the same time. She tried to stand, but her legs were too wobbly.

Izzy sat in the grass and pulled her legs to her chest.

She stared at the list in her hand then ripped it into the tiniest pieces possible.

She stood and threw the pieces into the air. A strong gust of wind took the pieces up and over the fence. They twirled and scattered into the field and trees beyond the cemetery.

Gone. Never to come back.

Izzy stared into the field then pulled the china dog from her pocket. The surface was smooth and cool as she touched it to her lips like she had so many times. She stuffed the precious dog into her pocket. She turned to walk away but stopped and returned. One more touch of the china dog to her lips, then she wedged it between the vase and the big stone. Her running steps kicked up dust as she ran from the grave before she could change her mind about leaving it.

Clouds flirted with the blazing sun in a sky that was still blue. Cicadas still buzz-clicked in the trees. And life in Taggert Creek, on its crooked plot of earth, was unchanged. Unchanged for all except the girl traveling through the cemetery gates.

This girl carried an ache that seemed smaller.

This girl with thoughts of the library, the smell of ink and paper, and which book to read first.